A PARTNER FOR PENNY

Penny had grown up with Christopher Lloyd and saw in him the older brother she'd never had. She was dismayed when he arrogantly expressed the view that she ought not to trust her new business colleague, Gerald Hart. But Penny was a fighter and opposed Chris by setting out to win Gerald as a partner both in love and business. When she was disillusioned, Chris was too big a man to say he'd told her so. Too late, Penny realizes the depth of her feelings for Chris.

PAULA FOREST

A PARTNER FOR PENNY

Complete and Unabridged

LINFORD
Leicester

First published in Great Britain

First Linford Edition
published 1997

British Library CIP Data

Forest, Paula
    A partner for Penny.—Large print ed.—
Linford romance library
    1. English fiction—20th century
    2. Large type books
    I. Title
    823.9'14 [F]

    ISBN 0–7089–5031–0

Published by
F. A. Thorpe (Publishing) Ltd.
Anstey, Leicestershire

Set by Words & Graphics Ltd.
Anstey, Leicestershire
Printed and bound in Great Britain by
T. J. Press (Padstow) Ltd., Padstow, Cornwall

This book is printed on acid-free paper

1

"**I** WON'T let you, Chris, never! You can't make me change my mind. I'm going to decide for myself."

Penny stood up, slight beside the tall, lithe grace of Christopher Lloyd. She was determined and, though his proudly-held head was unbending, she managed to look most dignified. Lounging arrogantly on the arm of the settee, Chris sighed:

"My dear girl, you're simply too young and inexperienced to handle this on your own. You're just a child — why you look no more than seventeen! You'd be wax in the hands of anyone who wanted to cheat you."

"Gerald doesn't want to cheat me; he loves me. And I'm not just seventeen. I'm the same age as you and well you know it! I wish I'd never told you now."

"You're rather a little idiot, you know, Penny." Chris drawled as he moved his lean muscular body restlessly.

"Can't you get it into your head that you're now a good catch for any man? Did this Gerald know about your inheritance before he declared his love?"

Penny's face had grown whiter throughout the argument and now her eyes, too big in the face that was tense with strain, flashed angrily. It was like being a child again as she gazed up into the stern tanned features — at the mouth already shaping its mocking smile. His crisp dark hair might be a little longer now, curling thickly into the nape of his neck, but essentially he hadn't changed a bit. He was just as hateful!

"Thanks! That's a very good opinion you have of me!"

"Oh, for God's sake!" he returned

impatiently. "Don't talk such a lot of rubbish. You make it all so personal! After all, I only offered to meet the fellow and discuss the business side of your relationship."

"I don't want you to meet him."

"O.K. There's nothing more to be said then."

"Nothing! I wish I hadn't come."

"But you did," Chris pointed out reasonably, "and since you're here I'll ask Molly to bring in the tea."

"Not tea! I couldn't touch a thing."

"Really!"

Tiny lines of amusement appeared at the corners of his eyes and Penny knew that he was remembering their younger days and countless invitations to tea that had always resulted in eating competitions. A mere girl, she had been determined not to be outdone in the numbering of scones, sausage rolls and cakes that could be consumed at one sitting. Then, they had been rivals in everything. Although he'd lived in the big house outside of the village and she in a cottage down in the vale, they had been companions from an early age. Their parents were friends and had agreed that the two should grow up together. So they had. But each, rebelling against constant recitals on the perfection of the other, sought to be leader in all things. Their childhood had been marked by contests, most of them, as Penny was reluctantly forced to admit, won by Chris. His superiority had been maddening at the time and now, as always, she felt that familiar urge to score off him. She, Penelope Janes, had always been in Christopher Lloyd's life, a toddler, a child and then a teenager. She had come back to him as a woman with a problem. To him, she was still Penny, the adolescent. He simply hadn't noticed that she'd grown up.

Despite their antagonism, he was the nearest she had ever had to a brother and she'd expected a sympathetic hearing if nothing else. All the way down from London she'd rehearsed what she would say to him. Silently, in her corner of the carriage, she'd gone over the words she needed to describe her love for Gerald. Unexpectedly, it mattered very much that Chris should think well of Gerald. She hadn't been prepared for his new worldliness, hadn't thought he'd accuse her of indulging in calf-love. Hers wasn't calf-love. Never had been. She was going to marry Gerald. Why should she let Chris fill her heart with doubts? He had been unerringly right when he'd suggested that Gerald's proposal came after the news of Grandma's will. But that was only because Gerald hadn't enough money to take on a wife at the same time as buying himself into the hotel business. With the money from her inheritance, Penny would be able to be an equal partner. Partner in all senses. How exciting it had seemed until Chris had started probing beneath the romance, searching for ulterior motives and laughing at love. Even now he was laughing at her, as Molly appeared in the doorway with the tea he'd ordered:

"So yours is the big romance!" he teased, "afternoon tea with big brother in his gloomy sitting room must seem tame in comparison!"

"Never tame! You're . . . you're . . ."

"Wet-blanketish?"

"Like a heavy-handed father with a child who forgot to wash her neck."

"And did you?"

"Oh Chris! All that was ages ago. I'm grown up now."

"Are you?"

Penny was not prepared for the sadness in his voice. The tone of lingering regret so moved her that she bent her head and picked up the silver tea-pot, pouring out the hot amber liquid into cups that reflected its warmth. This was the very first time she had taken charge of the tea pouring in Grange House. Before there had always been Chris's mother, a warm welcoming hostess. Her presence had spilled over into the rooms giving them an untidy comfort which radiated friendliness in what might otherwise have been austere grandeur. She and her husband had been killed in a car crash over a year ago. All that warmth and kindliness wiped out. Chris had not altered the colour scheme or the furnishings, yet the room had acquired a studied neatness, an elegant perfection. Penny had always loved this room and, for a moment, she forgot her own problems in remembering Mr. and Mrs. Lloyd. They, too, had been part of her growing up, part of the happiness of childhood. Like Grandma had been in her rambling cottage with its fires of logs and gleaming copper pieces. Nostalgia for the past darkened her large blue-grey eyes. She had no idea how wistful and lost she looked as she handed Chris the cup and saucer. For a second, their moods matched and Chris bent sympathetically towards her.

Then the door opened and Molly stood in the doorway, her lips pursed in disapproval. She had been with the family too long to stand on ceremony. "There's another visitor for you, Mr. Christopher. Another lady!"

She spoke as though accusing Chris of an orgy she could not bear to countenance. Penny giggled, part in relief as the mood relaxed and part in amusement that this tall, grey-haired woman should dare to criticise Chris.

"Oh, damn!" he exploded as though resenting an intrusion into their moment of privacy. The light of sympathy died in his eyes and, his face impassive as though the last few minutes had never happened, he said, "Oh, thank you. Show her in please."

"Shall I bring her through now or after Miss Penny's gone?"

"Now, of course."

There was, however, no need for Molly to show the visitor in. A tall, slim woman appeared in the doorway and announced herself in a deep dramatic voice. "Hello, darling. I'm back. Aren't you glad it didn't take as long as we thought?"

"Joanna! How lovely!"

In one stride he was by her side, gathering her hands into his own as she raised her face for a kiss. Penny was surprised to intercept a long, calculating look from those beautiful eyes as they regarded her across Chris's shoulder. They held more interest and awareness than Penny felt she warranted. After all, however friendly Chris was with this sophisticated vision, there was the bond of years between him and Penny. He was obviously aware of this himself, for he turned and introduced Penny as a childhood friend. She wished she could stretch up one cool hand in acknowledgement of the introduction, but she had just picked up a squishy chocolate cake and her fingers were sticky. She hoped that her brief nod in the newcomer's direction would cover her discomfort at being caught to her disadvantage, but Chris had noticed her lack of finesse with the gooey confection and tossed her his handkerchief with the suggestion that she mop up. Suddenly,

Penny was angry. Too well she sensed what was about to happen. Chris, aware of this glorious creature's pleasure in him, looked amused, relaxed. Penny was about to be written off as a nuisance, worthy of little notice. Defiantly, she stood up.

"I ought to go."

"Why: Are we neglecting you?"

"No, but you'd rather be alone."

"Would we indeed?" The amusement in his tawny eyes deepened and Joanna looked faintly discomposed as though his teasing of Penny signalled a closer friendship than she had realised. Her smile was patronising as she said, "You mustn't keep the child, Chris. She has obviously enjoyed her tea and now she wants to leave."

"Yes, it was a lovely tea. Thank you, Chris." She spoke like the dutiful schoolgirl they were both making her out to be. She did not want to intrude on their reunion, only to make a dignified exit. Standing, she just reached Chris's shoulder. His tall, lean figure stretched so much taller than she remembered and there was a suggestion of authority as he looked down on her.

"Will you come again, Penny?"

There was a silence. Penny turned and walked to the door. "No. I'm going back to London tomorrow."

"Then I'll come down to the gate with you."

Penny knew that she didn't want to hear any more of his arguments. If only he wouldn't automatically put her in the category of a silly girl. If only he would see her as she was, take her seriously. She would appreciate his help but not his condescension. She stood as tall as she could and said, "Don't bother, Chris. After all, I know my own way."

"Are you sure?" He bit back with double meaning. There could be no doubt that he referred to her proposed future with Gerald. Penny resisted the temptation to start her defence of Gerald all over again. What did it matter that this conceited bore thought that she was making a mistake? She didn't have to please him. They had grown apart. She would leave him to the smooth silk of his new love. His taste in girls had changed.

Penny didn't go straight home. She couldn't face her mother in this present mood. Mother always saw a great deal more than appeared on the surface. She would know that Chris and Penny had quarrelled and would guess it was over Grandma's cottage. Neither mother nor father had tried to influence Penny's decision. They would expect her to behave sensibly, knowing that she'd ask for their advice when she wanted it. Penny could visualise the veil of hurt that would shield her mother's eyes if she ever realised that her daughter could not bring herself to talk to her parents about Gerald. Not until she was certain. That was why she had gone to Chris, expecting help. Well, now she knew his opinion!

After leaving the big house, as she

had always affectionately called it, Penny took the hill road. She intended to climb to where she could look out over the peaceful vale of her childhood and then go down on the other side. This had been a favourite Sunday afternoon walk of village families, Penny's no exception. They'd usually managed to pick up Chris on the way and, sometimes, his parents as well. Mother and Mrs. Lloyd had gone to the village school together and their long friendship had dated from then. After such walks the two families would crowd into the Janes's tiny cottage for tea. Penny's father had never been as successful as Mr. Lloyd. He'd never ventured into the city to business each day. He'd stayed at home, ensconced in the little shed he'd turned into a study, trying to capture his dreams in words. Sometimes he was lucky and sold the results, but there was no steady income. Penny remembered her mother's anxious frowns and recalled how often she had hurried off in the mornings to help in one or other of the outlying houses. Now Penny realised how her mother had earned the money for school uniforms and other expenses, leaving her husband free to follow his creative whims. She must certainly have had reason to feel dissatisfaction with her way of life, yet Penny had no recollection of that. The atmosphere in their home had always been gay and welcoming. Shabby here and there, the cottage might well have been but Penny had loved her home. She had never felt critical of it when they'd returned after those long walks, even knowing that the Lloyds' house was grander and quite beautifully furnished. All friends in the cottage, she had felt comfortable there among familiar, precious things. She'd not wished for more from home. Only now she longed to be able to bring Gerald to a place like the one she'd just left. She conjured up a picture of herself holding his hand as they entered the gates and walked up the long drive to Grange House. She'd be proud to introduce him to her parents in such a place. He'd appreciate the quality of the building from another century with its modern way of life. Antiquity blended with easy living. Unobtrusive luxury in the midst of country pleasures. She felt guilty to think how easily she could have brought Gerald home if home had not been the shabby cottage in the village. And when her parents had visited her in her London flat she'd always managed to prevent Gerald from meeting them. They wouldn't like him, she knew.

Strange that she knew nothing of his background. She'd met him at the hotel where she'd been working as a receptionist. That had been part of her training in hotel management. She spent two days a week at college and the rest of her time acquiring practical experience. At first, she'd thought he was the manager until she realised that, like her, he was a trainee. This she'd found out from the other girls. He'd not given it away himself by look or word. His appearance was impeccable without being dashing. His manner was that of a superior, yet he could not be called bossy. Like a good manager, he was forceful when necessary and faded into the background when his presence wasn't needed. To Penny he had been Mr. Hart for months. He had given her the same brief smile in passing that he gave to all the girls — friendly yet aloof. Then she'd come off the evening shift one day to find herself faced with a torrential rainstorm. It had been in the summer at the end of a particularly hot day. Penny had not been prepared for the downpour. She'd stood in the foyer waiting for the storm to pass, vaguely uneasy because she knew that the staff were not expected to clutter the public rooms. It was then that the slim young man with smooth blond hair had paused at her side and offered her a lift. In his car she hadn't talked much, conscious that he was merely being kind to one of the employees. After all, he wouldn't have bothered with her if it hadn't been for the

16

storm. He'd left her outside of her flat and she'd run through the rain to reach shelter. When she'd turned in the hallway to look back, she'd been surprised to find he was still there, watching her. He'd waved then, before driving off and next morning he'd stopped at her desk with a friendly greeting.

It hadn't been until after she'd completed her stint as receptionist and moved on to another hotel as rooms supervisor that he'd asked her out. He'd phoned one evening to say that he'd been given tickets for a show and wondered if she would like to accompany him. Without friends in London, Penny had jumped at the invitation. Somebody she knew, somebody safe, had asked her out. She remembered how carefully she had dressed for that first date with Gerald. Her long dress had made her look taller, slimmer and more elegant. It was a lovely deep blue and, out of its high neckline, her head rose in charming relief with golden highlights gleaming from honey coloured curls. She still loved that dress because it had made her look attractive, helped to arouse Gerald Hart's interest. Even now she took extra pains over her appearance whenever she was going out with Gerald. Nothing like the faded jeans and loose sweater she was wearing this afternoon. It was no wonder Chris had seen her as the little girl of years ago. Her slight size and mop of unruly fair hair did nothing to make her look any older. Here, in her own village she felt comfortable in old clothes. She fitted them again with the same ease with which she had slipped back into the unhurried pace of country life.

Penny had walked across the top of the ridge that bordered the village without really noticing the view. It was enough that she was part of it. One blade of grass never stopped to watch another grow and so Penny blended into the landscape. She was a part of the singing summer grass and of the clear sky that curved above. At this moment she mattered in the pattern of the universe and was happy to have it so. Light of spirit, she came to the green boughed lane that made a tunnel of leaves into her grandmother's cottage. This had always been a magic entrance into mystic territory for Penny as a child. The sprites were alive in the form of shafts of sunlight filtering through moving leaves. Coming into the shade after the brightness, her eyes were bemused with tiny glints of light weaving some dance of their own. Penny waited for them to settle before feasting her senses on the sweet-smelling shrubs and flowers of the familiar garden. It was as she remembered it, yet now the weeds grew in thick profusion among Grandma's favourite flowers. The subtle perfume of herbs evoked again her grandmother's memory. Penny could see her still, sitting in a high-backed chair at the window, gazing out on the garden. For a moment the old wrinkled face lit up, as it had always done, to welcome the arrival of a favourite granddaughter. Then a jagged crack across the windowpane shrieked out of neglect and reminded Penny that her grandmother had gone for ever. Tears welled in her eyes. Here, to an old lady with love in her heart, she had been wont to bring all her troubles. Now she was alone. The rambling old cottage and its acres of orchard and woodland belonged to her, Penelope Janes. It would be an ideal place to live and Penny did not wish to abandon it to strangers. Yet a whole new life beckoned to her. Together, she and Gerald could start well up the ladder in the hotel business. With her money and his know-how, they could go far. With her money! That was the rub. Was it really possible that Gerald hadn't even considered marriage until after he'd heard of Penny's inheritance? Had she mistaken his attentions for love? There had been no doubt in her mind until she'd seen Chris. He'd sown the seeds;

hers was the harvest. Given the chance, would she have brought Gerald to meet Grandma? Would he have wanted to come?

These questions still tormented Penny when she travelled back to London the next day. Watching beloved landmarks disappear into the general greenness, her heart yearned to be able to return to the place of her birth. As green faded into red-brick and smoke-discoloured buildings she found herself thinking ahead to London. It was with mounting excitement that she saw the bright advertisements on station hoardings. They spoke of shows and city life. In vivid tones, they sang of a life with Gerald.

The train drew into Waterloo Station and her feet danced along the platform in anticipation. There was no one waiting at the barrier, so she turned into the road where she might catch a bus. There he was. Gerald was sitting in the open car, waiting for her. He wore sunglasses that made him seem just a little remote, a handsome stranger. The long shiny car and the assured young man took on a flamboyance that startled her after her days in the country. It came to her that Gerald was altogether different from Chris, his slender build and sensitive features giving him a boyishness that would always let him seem younger than his years. However, all comparison ceased when he saw her and opened the door of the car with a flourish. "Going my way?" he joked.

She tuned into his mood easily, replying lightly. "It depends how far you're going."

"All the way!"

"Good!"

"Then jump in," he encouraged as she still guarded her suitcase beside her on the pavement. She slid into the soft luxury of the car seat as he stored her luggage in the boot. When he climbed in beside her, she smiled her delight, "It's lovely to be back."

"Didn't you enjoy the countryside

and the peasants this time?"

His smile was indulgent, but she felt there was criticism of her in his patronising attitude towards her family. She tried to ignore the prickle of resentment at his words. "It's my home and I've always loved it."

"But you never expected to own property there. It must have been quite a change to return as the wealthy landowner."

Her frown must have told him that she was hurt by his manner, for he placed his hand lightly over hers and assured her. "I had no intention of sounding such a snob. I'm sorry, darling, but I've been so worried since you left."

"But why?"

"I thought you'd change your mind and decide you didn't like living in the city after all."

"You know how I feel about London."

"Yes, but it's only for a while, my sweet. If you decide to sell up and come into partnership with me, we'll settle for a country-house hotel in Devon."

"How lovely!"

"I thought you'd like the idea. But I was afraid you'd fall in love with the cottage and not want to sell it."

Her smile was rueful as she confided in him: "It doesn't seem right, somehow, selling Grandma's cottage. I — I wish I needn't."

His glance flicked to her briefly as he pulled up in the square where Penny had her second-floor flat. "Haven't you put it on the market?"

"Not yet. My mind was too full of doubts."

"Doubts about us?"

His voice grated as though he harboured feelings too deep to show. He opened the car-door for her with his usual impeccable good manners and handed her out of the car, but he seemed withdrawn and there was a faint droop of sulkiness about his mouth. Could he possibly be jealous — jealous of the countryside she adored?

They were quiet as they climbed the stairs to her flat. Gerald seemed impatient as Penny hunted in her bag for the key. Inside, he carried the case through to the bedroom while she stood in the centre of the big sunny room she called her lounge, and tried to feel at home. The colours she'd chosen as modern seemed strident against the memory of soft, blurred chintz. The wide spaces of the room needed filling with the clutter of life, with precious and well-loved pieces. Then Gerald came back and the room was right again. It suited the ambitious young man to whom roots were only a nuisance. He needed space to expand; there were places to go and he wanted to take her with him. Now he looked uncertain as if she had dealt him a real blow. Their eyes met and she read the entreaty in his. He could not beg, but he wanted her. Swiftly, she crossed to him and, once she had made the move, he held out his arms to take her.

They were together again. Nothing

else mattered. He bent his head and she felt his lips on hers. A surge of happiness thrilled through her and her eyes spoke for her. They were bright with love and hope. He smiled as he gazed down into their blueness. After a moment, he said, "Penny, I must ask you something."

"Yes, Gerry? What is it?"

He held her closer for a moment, then said, "Were you ever in love with your playmate in the country?"

"Playmate? What do you mean?"

"Chris somebody or other. You went back to see him, didn't you?"

"I did see him, yes. But I went back to see Grandma's cottage."

"But you do like him, don't you?"

She was a little surprised by this question. She did not reply but looked up at him, trying to read in his eyes the reason behind such a question. The expression in his lighter than blue eyes was unreadable. She longed to let her finger trace the outline of his handsome features, the sensitively shaped mouth, the slender curve of his throat, but he was pleading now: "Penny!" he said urgently, "You must answer me. Please!"

For the first time since she'd known him, Penny felt almost certain of his love. Softly, she asked, "Why do you want to know?"

"Because, until I know I won't have a minute's peace of mind. I need to know whether I've got a chance."

"Chris and I grew up together, Gerry. I used to spend a lot of time with him."

"And you saw him again this weekend?"

"Yes, but he's changed." She saw Chris again towering above her, his lean face rugged and his strong jawline emphasising an iron will.

"You still like him, though, don't you?"

"I'm not going back to him, Gerry."

"Not to the village?"

"It's his home too. I can't stop him being there."

"Then you won't keep the cottage near him, will you?"

"No I suppose not. Why should I?"

Gerald had almost won. He had only to convince her that he would be happy to fall in with all her wishes. She needed to be certain of his love.

"Have you any idea, Penny, how much I love you and want you? Have you?"

"I'm beginning to get the idea."

His hands moved up her back, warm and urgent, and his lips found hers with an insistence she could not deny. Into the silence she vowed that she would arrange to have her grandmother's cottage sold. Perhaps there would be no need to go back again. No need to meet Chris. She had her future with Gerald to look forward to.

"Yes, I know now and I know what to do," she whispered softly into Gerald's kiss.

2

LIFE rushed on again. There was so much to do, so much to plan. One day ran into another in a fever of activity. Gerald came and went, dashing in and out with news of hotels up for sale or proposed deals. Friends gathered in her flat for drinks or dispersed hastily according to their usefulness. New acquaintances were always ones who knew somebody with influence or who could arrange meetings. To Penny it was like a kaleidescope of bright fragments breaking and reforming into never to be repeated patterns. Against its heady excitement, her weekend at home assumed a new importance, like the still centre that could be depended on never to change.

There were letters from home, then letters back, with the feeling that she was betraying a trust. Her parents did not question her decision to sell Grandma's cottage but they were full of careful anxiety about her happiness. Then came that rare thing, a letter written by her father. Penny was surprised at how much more naturally he wrote to her than he could ever speak. Shy of the young woman who had come home when it suited her, full of her clothes, her hair, her romances, he now wrote to the girl Penny had been. Then, he had known her closely and intimately, had always understood just how she felt. He had been a refuge for Penny and Chris, had shared their happy times and soothed their fears. Her mother had banned her from her father's small outdoor sanctuary, but, seeing Penny and Chris approach, his face had always creased into a smile of welcome:

"Come in, my dears, come along in."

As she read his words, Penny heard again his deep voice falling with easy familiarity on her ears. She saw the privacy of that bright little room and remembered that she had something to tell him.

Gerald . . . No, she could not describe Gerald very well. She didn't know how to tell her father. Her pen faltered as she sought for words and her statements became bald and factual. Grandma's cottage must be sold. There was no question of keeping it. She and Gerald were going into partnership. Later they'd marry. She wrote the stark facts with regret, wishing she could draw close to her dear father with words. But she understood him too well. There was no way to ease the hurt she must cause him. He had asked her to go home and talk things over, but she could not promise that. There was so much to do in London.

Gerald planned to hold a party at Penny's flat. They must celebrate. Not their engagement. They'd decided not to get engaged. They were a modern couple. They didn't need the traditional symbols. They would celebrate their partnership, a business deal, properly drawn up. Two weeks ago they'd gone down to Devon to view a property. It was a country-house hotel. Not a comfortable chintzy one full of permanent old ladies but a fashionable place where well-known personalities spent their weekends. Gerald had fabulous ideas for extending its scope and, ever since their visit, they'd been signing documents and poring over plans. Penny scarcely knew what she signed but Gerald was good at finance and such like. She left him to cope. If she regretted that there were no cosy evenings spent discussing a future home, she didn't show it. She gave up the task of choosing curtains and colour schemes to an interior decorator Gerald happened to know. Between them, the two men considered the suite of rooms set aside for Penny and Gerald's private use as part of the whole. When Penny demurred, Gerald pointed out that she'd be able to give the place personality when she lived there. He needed to create the right atmosphere now, from the beginning. Avon House had a lot of potential and Gerald sought just enough professional advice to be confident of its future. Without the prospect of Penny's new-found wealth they would have been unable to arrange a mortgage. As it happened, there were no legal complications to their business partnership. They had plenty to celebrate.

The day of the party was a busy one for Penny. She spent the morning adjusting her flat to accommodate all the guests. In the afternoon she started to prepare food. She was busily but happily occupied when the phone rang.

"Yes?" Penny said, "Hello? Who is it?"

"It's me — Gerald. Penny, I must see you."

"Darling, you'll see me tonight. Come early before the others arrive."

Instead of agreeing, he asked, "Could

you come over now? I need to talk to you."

She swallowed before venturing: "Is something wrong?"

"Nothing at all that can't be put right, but it needs your signature."

"Can't it wait? I'm so busy."

"Whatever you're doing, this is more important."

"But the party!"

"I'll arrange some help for you."

"It's too late now."

"Not at all. I know just the person. He'll be glad to make an extra pound or two."

"But when?"

"When? Now. Please get ready to come. Then wait. When John arrives, leave him to cope and come on over."

"John?"

"Yes. You've met him. When you worked here. He's the tall dark student, helping in the kitchen."

"John? — sort of gawky looking? I think I remember."

"It isn't important," he cut her off.

"But your coming here is."

"Oh."

"Please don't be difficult about it. I'll be waiting in the lobby." then he added in an assuring whisper: "I love you."

She dressed carefully and was ready to leave when John arrived. He listened quietly to her directions, added a few suggestions of his own and was actually at work before he said, "I asked the taxi-driver to wait for you."

"You what?"

"Mr. Hart said I was to send you straight over by taxi."

"Oh. Thank you."

It seemed she had no choice. Indeed, Gerald was waiting for her in the lobby, apparently unable to do anything but pace up and down. "Oh, Penny, at last!"

"What is it, Gerald?"

He was already walking her to the lift when he said, "There's been a hitch. With the sale of the cottage."

"Oh."

"Your lawyer's here."

"Couldn't he have waited until Monday?"

"No. He needs your signature today and I'm afraid you'll have to go down for the sale."

"Oh, no!"

"I couldn't quite muster the courage to tell you on the phone, but you must go."

"Why can't he manage it without me?"

They were out of the lift and outside the door of Gerald's office when he held her by the arms and said urgently, "You will tell him you'll go, won't you? Promise."

"Is it so important to you?"

"Yes, it is. Or have you changed your mind about us?"

"No, I haven't changed my mind, but I didn't want to go back again."

"You needn't meet anyone. It might be better if you didn't. But say you'll go. Please."

"Of course, if I must."

"And promise not to let anyone

persuade you to change your mind."

"I won't change my mind."

"Come on, then."

He ushered her into the room where her grandmother's solicitor waited. The old man's wide brown face and thatch of thick white hair seemed ill at ease against the modern decor of the hotel. But the grey eyes were as sharp as ever as they smiled a greeting.

"Little Penelope!" he said softly and she was tempted to run to him, but Gerald's voice was curt:

"Miss Janes understands the importance of your visit, Mr. Limpeney. It was just her signature you needed, wasn't it?"

The great white head turned and directed a long questioning look at Penny. "I thought it best to come here, Miss Penelope, but could I talk to you alone for a moment?"

Gerald's impatience was scarcely hidden from Penny, who stared from one man to the other unable to understand their antagonism.

"Miss Janes and I are to be married.

There are no secrets between us."

"Is that how you want it, my dear?" the eyes were a little anxious now as they searched her face.

"Of course. You have something for me to sign?"

At once, the old man became business-like and produced papers from his briefcase. It took only a few minutes to conclude the matter and Penny wondered why there had been so much fuss. As the elderly lawyer turned to go, he asked, "You're coming back with me, aren't you, my dear?"

"Not today."

"But you'll come down for the sale? You are coming, aren't you, Penelope?"

"I'll come."

"Good girl. Come straight to my office, won't you? I'll be there waiting."

"Yes, of course."

His eyes just failed to meet hers as they said goodbye. As soon as he had gone, she turned a troubled face to Gerald, "I still don't understand."

"Obviously, he's been asked to talk to you, to try to persuade you to change your mind."

"I don't want to talk any more."

"Then don't."

"But — you said — "

"It was your signature that was important. Now you can forget it."

"Need I go back, then?"

"Just for the day. But there's nothing to worry about. Don't give in."

"Will he try to persuade me?"

"I think he knows it's useless."

"But I really don't understand."

"There's nothing for you to understand. Somebody's putting pressure on him to persuade you to hang on to that cottage. For their own ends, no doubt."

"But my parents would never do that!"

"Who else stands to gain?"

"Nobody, only me."

"You'll be better off with the money. It's already tied up in our hotel."

"I know and I'm pleased."

"Then go down for this sale and get

it all signed and sealed. You won't be divided then."

"I'm not divided. The party is to celebrate our union."

"Good girl! See you tonight, then."

Penny felt dismissed like an employee whose discussion had been cut short. As she left the building she thought how nice it would be when she and Gerry were working together again. She felt cut off from him lately, but she knew that he'd been very busy. In future she'd be able to take some of the responsibility from his shoulders.

Back at the flat she discovered that John was capable of preparing the party alone. His imagination had been at work and he'd wrought miracles in the flat. His touches had been few and quite simple but they'd transformed the room into the perfect background for a party. Feeling unwanted in her own kitchen Penny decided to take a bath. She luxuriated in the warm water and tried to smooth away all the tensions of the day.

Gerald arrived early for the party and took over from John. Penny would have liked to ask the young student to stay but Gerald was so brisk and business-like in his dealings with the lad that Penny felt both of them would have found such an invitation ludicrous. As things were, she and Gerry would have ten blissful minutes alone before the bell started to ring.

Penny wore a long slim-fitting dress of material so dark a green as to be almost black. To herself she called it forest black, for it was the exact colour of the secret glades she knew at home, glades where no sun shone and colour was only just distinguishable. On anyone else such a shade could have looked drab, but it was the perfect background for Penny's clear complexion and it taught the tints of her feathery blonde hair how to shine. She'd had her hair fashioned in the way Gerald liked it and she could tell from the look in his eyes that her appearance was right for the occasion. He mixed drinks for two glasses then handed one to her.

"Let's drink to success, darling."

"A successful party?"

"Better still, a successful partnership."

"To the future, then."

"To us."

His voice was low and attractive and, to Penny, those words were magic. She began to view the evening ahead with happy excitement. A thrill of anticipation took over from the tension she had been feeling. Gerald put on some music and held out his hand. She took it and they began to dance.

It was a crazy thing to do because, of course, the door bell shrilled through the romantic music. People had started to arrive. They came alone, in twos and sometimes groups of four or six, bringing gay chatter and amused laughter into the brightness of the room. Penny was happy to be with Gerald to receive them. Again and again, she left his side to show the girls where to leave their outer wrappings. She saw them this way, gay parcels waiting to reveal their splendour — an offering to the evening. She didn't tell Gerald. He'd laugh at such a fanciful idea. But her lips curled in merriment as she surveyed the scene. She moved among her guests easily and with grace, stopping to exchange a few words here or an introduction there. There was nobody she knew well enough to stop to talk to for long. She was happier on the move, taking in impressions of the evening. Dancing started, more of a close shuffle because of the space. Accepting congratulations on her own for the umpteenth time, Penny looked around for Gerald. He should share these good wishes. At the door he was greeting Ted and a friend. Penny knew Ted well but she'd never met this girl before. She was tall, almost as tall as Gerald, but dark and beautiful in a haunting way. There was an aura of mystery about her that made Penny stand still and watch. The girl and Gerald were laughing together in a way that suggested intimacy, standing close to form a striking picture. He was devastatingly handsome, fair as a shining knight, and she some wild, seductive creature. Why didn't Ted object to his girl making eyes at another man? The girl was interested in Gerald, that was for certain. Penny crossed to the trio and put a hand lightly on Gerald's arm. She needed to establish her right. With her coming an embarrassed silence fell on the little group. For a moment everything stopped and Penny felt that all eyes were on her. Ted was first to speak.

"Hello, Penny. I don't think you've met Laura, have you?" A long slim hand took Penny's and cool grey eyes surveyed her.

"Penny — I'm so glad to meet you at last. I've heard so much about you."

"Well, Ted's helped us a lot. He's bound to be biased."

"Ted? Oh, of course."

Penny got the distinct impression that Laura had not been referring to

Ted. Who else would have talked of Penny to this cool beauty? Gerald had slipped away to dispose of Laura's light coat. As he returned, Laura deliberately left Penny and went to meet him. Inside, Penny was furious. This girl had cut her, had shown a distinct desire to hurt her. Why? They'd never met before. She would claim Gerald and show Laura whose evening it was. There was no need. Gerald himself proved adept at bringing Laura and Ted together before sweeping Penny away into the centre of the dancers.

"Sorry about her, darling."

"Whoever is she?"

"Someone Ted met at a party. She's rather overwhelming, isn't she?"

"She seemed to know you."

"Yes, we've met but I've always managed to avoid her talons."

"Oh?"

"She's using Ted. It isn't him she wants. She's after some bigger fish."

"You, for instance?"

"Don't be silly, darling."

There was no doubt though that the calculating glance of the lady Laura was often on Gerald's form. Her eyes seemed to follow him wherever he and Penny went. Impervious to it Gerald stayed attentively at Penny's side. Never before had he hovered like an adoring slave. He seemed intent on demonstrating his devotion, and Penny loved it. They danced, they circulated talking happily and they sat drinking. Always together. Gerald wove a magic circle round Penny, letting people in and out at his own desire, but never letting it be broken by sight or sound of Ted and Laura. The evening was a success; their party was a ball. Penny was a princess who needn't fear midnight. Prince Charming had the future under control. Happiness was now. The evening passed in a whirl of pleasure with the promise of love to come. It wasn't until she saw Ted leaving with another girl that Penny realised Gerald had left her side. By now she was in a mist of confused anticipation. She returned Ted's farewell wave, concluding that Gerald would be in the little hallway to see Ted off, then made for the bathroom. As she passed her bedroom door she noticed a couple silhouetted against the window. There was a street-light opposite that window and nobody had drawn the heavy curtains. Penny grinned impishly as she passed. That loving pair obviously didn't realise how easily they could be seen. How funny!

From inside the bathroom she could hear their voices, raised voices. One was Gerald's. She couldn't distinguish the words they were speaking but it was a quarrel. Not the quarrel of strangers finding themselves at loggerheads but an intimate quarrel, like a lover's tiff. Who was Gerald quarrelling with so violently? Penny strained to hear what they were saying but it was no good. Her head buzzed with noises from the party and she couldn't pick out a word of Gerald's argument. At last, she heard him bang out of the room and so she left her hideout and went into the bedroom to powder her nose. Laura was there. She was gathering up her coat and smoothing her dark hair. Her eyes did not reflect the smile on her lips as she said:

"I've enjoyed meeting you. Thank you for inviting me."

Penny refrained from pointing out that she had not asked the other girl. There was no excuse for rudeness. In any case, she had no reason to upset her even if she did feel an instinctive dislike for her. She wanted her out of the flat now so she asked: "Are you leaving now?"

"Why? Don't you trust me?"

"Why shouldn't I? I simply inquired when you planned to leave."

"I don't plan to go anywhere at the moment, thank you." It was then that Gerald came back, in time to hear Laura's deliberate insult. His face whitened to discover Penny in the room but he tried to smile.

"There's a taxi waiting outside, Laura."

"And if I don't choose to go?"

For a moment the air was taut with unspoken tension, then Gerald said, "We shan't throw you out of course."

His smile was sickly, and Laura laughed, "Watch him when he smiles Penny. He's up to something and it will pay you to find out what."

Penny looked from one to the other, wondering what all this was about. Into the pause, distinct and uncomfortable, Laura hissed, "Your darling lover wants to throw me out this minute. Do you want to know why?"

"Laura!"

Gerald shouted her name and, as if he had hit her, Laura stopped and stared at him. Her eyes were pleading and Penny saw the shimmer of tears. The words were for Gerald, not Penny, when she said, "I'm sorry. Have I messed things up for you as well?" The capitulation was complete. In the face of it, Gerald was magnaminous.

"Don't worry. I'm sure it will all work out for you. Now let's get you into that taxi."

Penny watched them go, Gerald supporting the drooped head on his shoulder. Then she waited, waited for Gerald to come back and explain.

It was a long wait because Gerald returned to a round of socialising. He offered drinks and accepted congratulations with a set smile on his face. Penny joined him, hovering at his side to pick up the crumbs of goodwill being showered with the farewells. Again and again, she heard the name of Laura mentioned. The dark beauty seemed to have caught the imagination of all. Ted was called all kinds of fool for preferring to leave with the mouse-like little girl he'd apparently picked up at the party. Fancy daring to leave Laura alone! A woman scorned! She'd find some way of retaliating.

Penny could not forget that the anger in those eyes had been for Gerald. Where did he come into all this?

She had to wait until the last guest had gone before she could confront him. Even then, he busied himself with emptying ashtrays and stacking up plates. Penny came straight to the point.

"Gerald, how well do you know Laura?"

"As well as everybody else, darling."

"But why have I never met her before?"

"She's not your type, love. I didn't want Ted to bring her tonight but he insisted."

"More likely she did!"

"Perhaps, but what have Ted's girlfriends and their bickering to do with us?"

"I have a feeling Laura has a lot to do with you."

"Really, darling! You're dramatising everything. What could there possibly be between me and that girl?"

Penny paused, trying to believe him, but she had to ask: "What were you quarrelling about?"

"Quarrelling? Come now, it's your imagination again!"

"No, Gerald! I heard you. In the bedroom."

The slightly superior smile of indulgence left his face. He poured himself a drink and Penny noticed that, for the first time, he didn't ask what she'd like.

"What exactly did you hear, Penny?"

Beneath the honeyed smoothness of his question there was the rasp of ruthlessness that she'd noticed in his dealings with others. She wasn't sure how far she could push him.

"I — I heard you quarrelling."

"Are you sure?"

"Quite sure, Gerald. I'm not a fool and you were shouting at each other."

"What did we say?"

The question hit her, making her realise that she hadn't, in fact, heard a word that she could quote back at him.

"The party muffled what you said but I know you were having a row."

"Oh, Penny, my little darling, you've upset yourself over nothing."

"Nothing?"

"I know we shouted at each other but I didn't want you to be worried."

"Worried about what?"

"Well, I didn't like the way Laura was treating Ted."

"Everybody else seemed to think it was the other way round."

"Yes, but that's how she works. It was obvious from the start that she was going to make a dead set at somebody. That's why I kept out of her way."

"You?"

"I see I'll have to tell you now."

"Tell me what?"

"Sit down, here on the settee with me."

He led her to the sofa and his arms. He kissed her warmly and searchingly until she responded. Holding her close, he explained: "I used to date Laura myself."

"Oh!"

She tried to loosen his clasp but he

wasn't going to let her go.

"Don't mind so, sweetheart. It was before I met you."

"She's very beautiful."

"Yes, but she's hard. She fights to the kill. That's why I wanted to help Ted."

"Ted?"

"Yes. Tonight, in him, I recognised myself when I was in Laura's sway. I tried to help Ted lose her without losing his pride."

"The other girl?"

"Yes. It worked. Only, afterwards, Laura cornered me and accused me of manoeuvring it."

"That's why you quarrelled?"

"Yes. She was mad with fury."

"I heard her."

"I'm truly sorry about that, my darling. I didn't mean to hurt you."

His soft, gentle kissing of her ear lobe and throat stopped her from crying. She'd been so silly. Gerald didn't like women to be all emotional. She'd got worked up for nothing.

"I'm sorry, Gerald."

"Don't let's talk any more," he pleaded.

"But I nearly spoilt everything!"

He had been scared, had nearly lost Penny, her money, the hotel and everything. He could now afford to be generous. He cradled her head with his hands.

"Look," he said softly, "I love you."

Quite simply, Penny was his again. She put her arms around him and turned her face up to his to speak. But there was only silence as his mouth came down demandingly on hers.

3

PENNY felt the prick of tears as she gazed round the familiar garden. All the sweetness of its past had been destroyed, trampled by heavy feet. Neatly piled and tied books and heaps of old-fashioned utensils crushed the grass. Everything had been sorted into lots and gave up Grandma's secrets to the strangers who prowled the house and gardens. The old cottage was in a very bad state of repair. Her grandmother had let it go in later years and the place had stood empty since her death. Its air of sad neglect made Penny feel guilty. She shouldn't have come here today, not just before the sale. She found the place disturbing. It was so different now and yet, in essence, it seemed to have changed so little from those days when she had run excitedly over the soft grass following Chris inevitably, with Grandma's indulgent eye on them. In the orchard they had climbed trees with little regard for the fruit they were to bear and their careless play had sent the cherry blossom showering over the long grass.

As if her memories had conjured him, Chris came slowly through the tunnel of greenery that shaded the gate. Penny saw him look at the cottage as if there were some deep and painful longing in him, but she must have imagined most of it for, as he caught sight of her, he called cheerfully, "Remembering the old days, Penny?"

"Yes — it's this place. I always loved it and yet now it's so sad somehow."

"Perhaps it doesn't like being deserted."

"Idiot!" she smiled. "How can a house know whether it's being deserted?"

"What a question, Penny! You, of all people, used to understand such things."

"Childish things. I've changed now."

"What a pity! There used to be a charm about you that bewitched me. Like the magic you believed in then. You used to call this your own special magic place."

"I don't remember it quite so — so sad."

"It's just the same, Penny. It's you who've changed."

"And so have you," she retaliated quickly.

"But you've let city living blind those lovely eyes."

"And you?"

"Basically I'm the same. Like this house is beneath the surface of its sorry state."

"And so am I. I can't help it that I must sell. I don't have any choice."

"Really!"

"Please, Chris — don't fight. Not here — not now,"

"Fight? Really, Penny! How much have you grown up?"

"All right, Chris. You think I'm still a child, but I do know what I'm doing."

"I hope so, Penny. I sincerely hope so."

He sounded so serious that she turned her head again to look at him, trying to read the expression on his face.

"Let's go down into the orchard," some imp of mischief prompted her to suggest.

"Tree-climbing?" he asked. "You still remember that?"

"Of course. I remember so much. They were such good days."

Her eyes were misty with half-remembered pleasures but he cut into her nostalgic dream abruptly.

"Surely you have good times to come?"

"Yes, but I'll never forget the lovely times here."

"You will — you must."

"And what about you, Chris?" she asked quietly.

"Well, what about me?" he drawled lazily.

"You've changed so, Chris. I can't

get near you any more."

There was a plea for understanding in her voice which he ignored. He gazed down at her, thumbs hooked carelessly into the band of his well-cut trousers, his lean face stern and thoughtful. "Maybe you've outgrown our togetherness, my sweet."

"I thought we'd always be friends."

"Is that possible?"

"Of course."

"Would Gerald understand our friendship?" he asked blandly. "Would he believe in its innocence?"

"Why not?" she demanded, realising as she spoke that Gerald would hate to know that she'd met Chris again.

"Why not indeed? But would he?"

She was saved from answering by the arrival of the same young woman who'd come to Grange House while she was at tea there. She strolled up to Chris and took his arm possessively.

"Sorry I'm so late, darling."

All the antagonism left his face which relaxed into a smile as he turned to greet the newcomer. "Joanna! You made it!"

"I knew you wanted me to help."

"Yes. You're so much better at valuing this stuff than I am."

His gesture indicated the contents of Grandma's cottage and Penny hated him that he could view such things merely as items in a sale. Had he no memory? No hankering for the days long since past and left in the mists of time? He was insensitive. Even his voice grated as he broke into her train of thought: "I believe you two have met before."

"Yes, of course." The smart young woman at his side would have dismissed Penny instantly except that she seemed to derive some pleasure in probing to see how deep a wound was left.

"You're selling, I believe?"

"Yes, I must."

"What a pity. There's some lovely stuff here."

"I know."

"One could do so much with the house too."

Chris interrupted her to ask: "Have you had any more ideas about the renovation?"

"Oh yes . . . " Her voice lowered dramatically and she and Chris were locked in quiet concentration of the house they'd come to view. Penny wandered away from them, back into the cottage. She glanced at her wristwatch and decided to go back to the solicitor's office. There was an hour before the sale. She could conclude her business in time to catch the late afternoon train. She couldn't think what had possessed her; coming to the cottage had been a mistake. For a whim, she'd broken her promise to Gerald. He'd begged her to go only to Mr. Limpeney's office and she'd agreed not to see anybody else, not even her parents. There'd been no definite idea in her mind of disobeying Gerald when she'd woken early and decided to catch the first train. In the golden haze of early autumn the village had seemed half asleep when she'd arrived. She had felt glad to be back and had wanted to walk and breathe in the tranquillity for ever. She had not at first been aware of the direction of her walk. Then she had entered the tunnelled path to her grandmother's cottage, her cottage now. Browsing among the objects for sale she'd told herself that it would be nice to find a little keepsake. Every item, large or small, was dear to her, too dear to sell and yet she could find nothing that Gerald would like too. She had spent longer than she should have done at the cottage. People were arriving now. Should her parents come they would be hurt to find her here with out their knowledge. She'd had no intention of meeting Chris either. He'd unsettled her. He appeared to disapprove of her relationship with Gerald yet he had his own romance with Joanna. Penny supposed it was a romance. When she'd mentioned it to Chris, his brows had arched with amusement and surprise. "She's out of your class, Penny!" he'd quipped and Penny had thought that Chris approved the cool beauty of the other girl. No wonder he still saw Penny as a child. It was silly to let that bother her. Gerald didn't treat her as a child. She let her mind wander to the long evenings through which they had planned and dreamed. There was no doubt now that Gerald loved her and wanted her. The qualities she loved in Gerald — his boyish ambition, his acquired worldliness, his willingness to say what pleased her — were all missing in the kind of man Chris had become in recent years.

Aching for Gerald in a way that came as a shock to her, Penny grew impatient of the village and the cottage. She dealt briskly and quite abruptly with Mr. Limpeney, giving him no opportunity for the quiet chat she knew he had in mind. No one was going to make her change her mind. She felt shame surge through her that she had let nostalgia take hold of her. She had tried again to make her peace with Chris when it was Gerald who had done so much for her. She should be grateful for the help he had so freely given her. She should be hurrying back to him, not deliberately wallowing in memories.

When Mr. Limpeney had reshuffled all the papers and expressed a certain satisfaction that Penelope had made a good deal, she hurried to contact Gerald. She would have given anything to be able to run to him, to feel his arms about her. The telephone was a poor substitute. Gerald sounded so remote. She was aware of a deep stab of disappointment. What she had expected she did not know. Certainly not this cool line of questioning that might have come from a stranger. He discussed the details of the sale with the detachment of a lawyer and it wasn't until he'd heard all that his voice relaxed into its familiar intimate tone. "Good girl, Penny, you've done well."

"I'm glad it's all over now."

"Yes, you won't need to go back again, so I'm glad too."

"But Gerry! The wedding!"

"Wedding, darling? But all our friends are here in London. You're not planning to drag them all down into the country, surely?"

"Well, I suppose not."

"That's the idea! You're a girl after my own heart, honey."

"Shall I see you tonight?"

"Of course. Unless you're too tired."

"Never too tired to see you, Gerry."

"That's my girl! You'll come back tonight, then?"

"Yes."

"There's one thing that's different. I've got to do the evening shift, so I can't see you till ten o'clock."

"Shall I meet you at the hotel?"

"No, I'll come to your flat."

"See you at ten, then."

"I'll be counting the minutes, my darling."

Whatever else he said was lost in the

surge of excitement Penny felt to be going back to him. Tonight they'd be together again, just the two of them. There was time to get back to London and have her hair set. She would look her loveliest. She had so much to offer him that the money from the sale was unimportant. It would help their future and they were the future — Gerald and Penny. There was everything to look forward to.

When Penny, wearing a soft dress of duck-egg blue, opened the front door at ten o'clock it was Ted and not Gerald who stood there.

"Ted!" The name escaped her almost involuntarily so great was her surprise at seeing him there. He shifted uneasily from one foot to the other then asked:

"Can I come in for a moment, Penny?"

Remembering her manners, Penny smiled a welcome and stepped to one side. "Of course, Ted. Come in."

His dark, craggy face looked older than she'd imagined him to be, yet at the same time he managed to look as lost as a small boy.

"What are you doing here, Ted? I was expecting Gerald."

"I know."

The directness of his remark and the way his eyes swept over her fragile prettiness made her very conscious of the effort she had made for Gerald tonight. She felt the warmth of a blush steal up into her face. Yet there was no need to explain to Ted why she wanted to look especially lovely. After all, it hadn't been him she'd been expecting. Something in his manner made her feel sorry for him in spite of her own disappointment. He was so ill at ease.

"Would you like a drink, Ted?"

"Please — and you'd better have one yourself."

"If it will make you feel happier, all right."

She crossed to the small drinks cabinet she'd had installed for Gerald's sake. There was whisky there and sherry, but little else. She poured

Ted a whisky with dry ginger then put the rest of the bottle of ginger into a glass for herself. It looked potent enough! She didn't much care for whisky herself.

Once he had the drink in his hand, Ted gained enough confidence to say: "I'm sorry, Penny. I know you were expecting Gerald, but he asked me to come instead."

"You? Why?"

"He can't make it tonight."

"Oh! But why didn't he phone? Why bother to send you over here?"

"I thought it best to come."

"You thought?"

Penny's knees were trembling now so she sat down suddenly on one of the easy chairs before she continued: "Has anything happened to Gerald?"

"No. He's fine."

"Then is he working?"

"No. He finished at six o'clock."

"Six o'clock! He told me ten. What's happened then? Why all the mystery?"

"I don't know why he finished earlier

than he told you, but I do know where he is."

"Then tell me."

"He's at the hospital."

"The hospital! But you said he was all right."

"Yes, he is."

"But the hospital? Can we go to him now? I'll get changed and we'll go."

"No, Penny! He's not ill."

"An accident, then?"

"Yes, but not to Gerald."

"Who? Who's hurt? You must tell me."

"It's Laura."

"Laura! But I don't understand."

"Laura tried to commit suicide tonight. Gerald found her and took her to hospital."

"Gerald found her! Found her where?"

"She was in her flat, I believe. I only knew about it when Gerald rang from the hospital. He asked me to come round here to keep you company."

"Company!" She almost spat the word at him. Why was he here keeping her company when Gerald was at the hospital with his girlfriend? But, then, Laura wasn't Ted's girlfriend any more, was she? Perhaps it was because of him she'd tried to commit suicide. He'd left her on her own at the party, hadn't he? But where did Gerald fit into this? Why should he be with Laura? She tried to get Ted to answer some of the questions that filled her mind.

"Ted, what would Gerald have been doing at Laura's flat?"

"I don't know, Penny."

"Did she send for him?"

"No. I believe she was unconscious when he found her."

"Will she die?"

"I don't think so. She had regained consciousness when he phoned."

"How do you know?"

"He told me that she wouldn't let him leave her."

"She wouldn't let Gerald go?"

"That's what he said."

"But — but they're nothing to each other!"

"They used to be very good friends, Penny. Didn't you know?"

She was quick to leap to Gerald's defence: "Yes. Gerald told me about it. But it's all over now."

"Let's hope so."

There seemed little else to say or do except wait. Penny wasn't even sure why they waited, but she made coffee and they sat in silence as her world seemed to crumble about her. She slipped away to change into something more casual, trying to destroy every reminder of the romantic evening that should have been. Ted didn't offer to leave and when, after midnight, the doorbell rang she knew it was Gerald. Penny was relieved to hear it, to break the blankness, but she didn't really want to open the door to him. Tonight he had let her down badly and she felt childishly that she should keep him waiting, punish him. However, she crossed to the door and opened it. Gerald's face at once surprised and alarmed her. It had gone white and his rather weak chin seemed tremulous as a tearful child's might be. There were no tears in his eyes, though. They were haggard and strained and, looking at him, Penny felt her anger evaporate into sympathy.

"Well, what's happened?" she asked as soon as the door of the flat closed behind him. "Is she all right?"

"For now," he answered abruptly and went straight to the cabinet where he poured himself a whisky. He didn't ask if he may and he didn't offer the others a drink. Penny and Ted looked at one another, for a second united in their annoyance with Gerald's calm manner. Surely, he owed them both an explanation! It was Ted who exploded first.

"You're being damned mysterious, aren't you? I came over to Penny as you asked. You could at least tell us what's going on."

"I'm sorry. Forgive me, but I've been so anxious."

"The hell you were! But why you?"

Again it was Ted who pressed the questions, but it was at Penny that Gerald had gazed when he'd begged to be forgiven. She sensed some deeper mystery behind Laura's suicide attempt. She had trusted Gerald implicitly but had she been rash to trust him so much? She had to find out and to get Gerald to confide in her she had to persuade Ted to leave.

"Ted, Laura's not dead. Can't the explanations wait until tomorrow?"

"Tomorrow? What the bloody hell have I given up tonight for?"

"Given up?"

"I'm not being rude to you, Penny," he said, "it's not that you're not all right but I did have an important date tonight."

"With Laura?"

"Laura be damned! Last time we met we quarrelled. She knew all about my girlfriend. It wasn't me who upset her, if that's what you're thinking."

"Then why did you come here?"

"For Gerald. I owed him. But not

now." He turned to Gerald: "All square now, mate?"

"All square Ted. Thanks."

So Gerald had been in a position to force Ted to come to her tonight. And his admission that Ted had paid any debt was all that was needed to send Ted away.

"I won't stay any longer," he said, "but you will be in touch, won't you, Gerald?"

"Yes, all right."

It was obvious to Penny that the casual words covered an unspoken agreement between the two men. Gerald had managed to convey to Ted that whatever had happened could be explained. Apparently satisfied, Ted left and, after he had gone, Penny determined to discover the truth.

"Gerald, will you please be frank with me? If you know why Laura tried to commit suicide, tell me now."

"Sorry to be difficult, Penny love, but I'm so worried."

"About Laura?"

"About what she's trying to do."

"To kill herself, you mean?"

"Not just that. She's using these threats of suicide to tie me to her."

"But why?"

"I told you we'd been friends?"

"Yes."

"Well, I met her again the day after our party."

"Oh!"

"She seemed upset and nervous. I asked her what was the matter but she wouldn't say."

"But she wanted you to meet her again?"

"She said I must meet her or I'd regret it for ever afterwards."

"And what was it all about?"

"She still wouldn't say but when I told her I wasn't going to deceive you she burst out with 'Penny'll have to face the truth. Why should I protect her'? so I told her I wouldn't meet her again. I said quite clearly 'We're finished, Laura, we're finished'."

So there had been more between

Laura and Gerald than he'd ever admitted. There had to be an affair to finish. He'd made it clear now. Gerald, as if not caring that he'd given so much away, continued: "If you're imagining that Laura tried to kill herself because of a row between us, I'll tell you now. There was something else on her mind before we quarrelled."

"Something else?"

"Yes. I didn't know then. I just sensed that something was wrong."

"But you know now?"

"Yes, she told me tonight. She told me why she tried to kill herself."

For a while he didn't try to enlarge on it. He sat with his head in his hands as if he still needed to decide whether to tell Penny or not. At last, without looking up, he said: "Laura was pregnant. That's why she did it."

"Poor thing!"

Penny's sympathy was genuine. Now, she could understand why Gerald had felt that he must stay with her. Was there no one to look after her? This baby must have a father too.

As if following her train of thought, Gerald mumbled, "All right. Don't rub it in."

"You mean? No you can't!"

"Yes. I'm the father. I can't desert her now, Penny. Everybody will ask about the father. Admit, you were wondering about him yourself."

"I suppose I was but I didn't know then that it was you. It doesn't make sense to me." She spoke plaintively, longing for him to deny it, to tell her that this whole evening had been some kind of charade and not true at all. She wouldn't question the cruelty of his joke if only he'd admit that it was a joke. Almost in answer to her silent plea, Gerald crossed to the sofa where she sat and pulled her into his arms. "Penny, this isn't the end of us, is it? You'll stand by me, won't you? You did say you loved me."

"Yes, Gerald, but everything seems so muddled now. How can you marry me when Laura is expecting your child?"

"I can't."

"You mean she must come first?"

"She said so tonight. She'll try to take her life again if I give her up. Next time she may succeed."

"But that's blackmail!"

"Yes, but Laura always gets her own way. It's not just the baby. Any other time she'd get rid of it. But this time it gives her the chance to trap me."

"How can she make you do what she says?"

"First there was you. She threatened to tell you the truth. I couldn't bear that, to see the hurt in your eyes."

"But I know now."

"And how I wish I could have saved you this evening. I didn't want you to know I'd been unfaithful."

Unfaithful! Yes, he had. It must have been since their understanding. Laura hadn't looked particularly pregnant at the party. Some time, when he'd been planning a future with her, Gerald had made love to Laura. Perhaps it wasn't just an isolated incident They could have been lovers all the while. Then why should Gerald have begged Penny to marry him? What was it he wanted of her?

"Penny, I've been trying to tell you ever since I came in tonight but with little success. I was a fool, Penny, a fool, and I'm sorry, deeply sorry."

"A fool to ask me to marry you or a fool to fall for Laura? Which, Gerald?"

There was no answer and Penny got the feeling that she was being weighed in the balance. Gerald sat close to her but now his head was buried in his hands.

"Penny, Penny," he groaned in despair. "I love you, damn it. I won't let you go."

It wasn't particularly easy for Penny to be cruel, but her own need was to discover the truth. "If you love me, Gerald, then how did this happen?"

"How, you ask! It happened because I love you."

"But why?"

"You went away for the weekend — down into the country. I knew you would be with your old playmate and I needed company."

"Company yes, but did you have to go so far?"

"So far," he mocked her angrily. "Don't tell me your childhood pal never made love to you!"

"Gerald, how could you!"

Penny's face was a study of startled surprise and anger. Did he really think of her like that?

"Oh, Penny!" he mocked. "Is he such a callow youth to be taken in by your looks of innocence?"

After a long silence she managed to reply and her voice sounded stilted and slightly remote even to her own ears. "Whatever happened at any time between Chris and me isn't your business any more."

"Any more! Was it ever? That was the trouble all the time. You were so cool, so self-sufficient. How could I tell you'd still be mine once you were back in that village of yours."

"I'd promised."

"Promised! How was I to know whether you'd have second thoughts? Well, I didn't sit inside worrying. I rang Laura and we went dancing. Then, I took her home and she asked me in for a drink." Quietly but firmly Penny interrupted: "Spare me the details, Gerald. I've heard enough."

"Enough! You don't want to hear how Laura and I made love? Weren't you doing the same thing down in the country? Why hide it now?"

Penny whitened and her head swam. She could not believe that Gerald was saying these things.

"You can't mean all this?" she whispered at last, her eyes darkening with disbelief, but Gerald had no intention of sparing her.

"Don't play the innocent with me, Penny. Didn't you discover that there's fun in numbers too?"

This was the man she'd expected to

marry. Her voice was pitched low in an effort at control: "Don't taunt me, Gerald," she pleaded. "I'm friendly with Chris that's all. You know very well that I've never slept with any man."

"I know nothing of the sort — only that you assumed a virginal outrage every time I tried to touch you."

All Penny's illusions were being roughly swept away. She struggled to achieve something of their former understanding.

"But I — I thought you wanted me as your wife, Gerald. Did you just want me to give in to your lust? Was that all?"

Then she stopped, a hand to her mouth, as a bitter laugh of realisation raked her throat.

"What a fool I am!" she exclaimed. "It wasn't just a physical attraction, was it You could get practically any woman if you wanted her. But you had to promise me marriage because you needed my money. Not only the money! You needed me too, to help run the hotel."

"Stop it!" Gerald took her by the shoulders and spun her round to face him. "You don't know what you're saying," he snapped.

"But I do! You talked of love and asked me to marry you for the sake of your hotel, not because you cared for me."

Instantly, his arms crushed her to him and his mouth found hers. "I do love you, Penny. You must believe me."

"But there's Laura," she whispered, her eyes begging him to deny it so that she could give in to the ardency of his embrace. His passion could sweep everything aside but she had to know that he would be true to her. He looked at her for a long moment as if he could consume her with his desire, but, when she didn't give way to the weakness that swayed her, he loosened his hold. Mutely she beseeched him with her huge pleading eyes. Even now she would be his but there must be no more Laura.

His passion gave way to a sulky sadness as he said, "I don't deserve you, Penny. You were right when you said I needed you. I still do but I can't marry you."

She felt stunned. What more did he want of her, then? Why the torment of begging her to love him when his loyalties were with Laura?

"Believe that I need you, Penny. You must always be near me."

"But not as your wife?"

"I'm sorry, my love, but I asked Laura to marry me tonight."

"Then it's all over. You'd better go."

"I'm not giving you up, Penny. Not that easily. I can't let Laura kill herself but I need you to help me. My life will be ruined unless you stick by me."

Someone other than Penny seemed to have taken over, someone so calm that Penny marvelled how easily Gerald could be sent away.

"It's over — finished," she said gently as if talking to a child.

"No!" he shouted, trying to accomplish by anger what he had failed to do by reason. The stranger who controlled Penny showed him to the door. Something in her manner forced him to go.

"Tomorrow, I'll see you tomorrow, Penny."

"Don't come, Gerald. It would be a wasted visit. There's nothing more to say."

"But there is! There's so much."

"Goodbye, Gerald."

She didn't wait to hear whether he replied. Once she'd propelled him through the door she pulled it shut and locked it. Caution kept her at the door in case he decided to knock or try to open it. But Gerald had accepted his defeat, for one night at least. She heard his footsteps going down the stairs.

Alone, Penny could let the cool

stranger go. There was no more need for pretence. Earlier she had rushed back to London to a life full of promise but now the desolation was too deep for tears. Her whole body trembled and she felt sick with shock. Gerald had only ever said he loved her to save her pride. He was a fortune-hunter, like Chris had said, and she had backed him into a corner when she'd expected marriage. He'd promised what she wanted and probably would have kept his word if Laura hadn't trapped him. He had made it easy for Laura to trap him, though. Had he wanted her all the time?

Penny tortured herself with thoughts until sleep came with some relief. In the morning she clung to the blackness that was sleep, sinking back into it again and again until she had to leave the sweet oblivion it offered and face the day. She longed for Gerald to ring, just to hear his voice, but knew that it would be no good. It was not a nightmare to be shaken off. She started to dial the number to ring Chris but her pride stopped her. He'd told her so all along. She had been just a child after all and now she had to grow up on her own.

4

THE weeks that followed were a haze for Penny, a haze into which Ted's face floated endlessly. It was a nice face, bespectacled and anxious. He, not Gerald, turned up daily at her flat. His cause, though, was not his own. He came to plead for Gerald. Sometimes Penny sent him away, sometimes she listened to him because it filled the blank between work and sleep and, often, she was out. When she was out, it was to avoid Ted and his entreaties on Gerald's behalf. She had nobody else to meet and she didn't feel like eating out alone. So, she walked. She walked the long pavements and didn't notice that there was no view.

From Ted she learned that Laura was out of hospital and that the baby was unharmed. That wasn't fair. She had tried to kill herself and hadn't even harmed the unborn child who had a hold over Gerald. One evening, in a sombre mood, Penny said as much to Ted. He wasn't surprised at her observation but added: "She'd have got rid of it if she'd wanted to, like the others."

"Others — "

"She's been pregnant before. She's never thought of having the baby before, though."

"Then why now?"

"Perhaps it was to keep Gerald, but she's never wanted marriage before, either."

"Would Gerald have married her before, Ted?"

"Well, it was Laura who always scoffed at the very idea."

"Why should she want him now, then?"

"A whim, maybe. Or out of spite. Spite's most likely, knowing Laura. She doesn't want you to have him."

"She hardly knows me!"

"But she's enjoying hurting you and him."

"Is he hurt?"

"You know he is, Penny. I've been telling you. He'll never manage without you. He really needs you — more than ever now."

"Then why doesn't he give Laura up and come back to me?"

"Give Laura up! Nobody gives Laura up. She isn't that kind of girl."

"I can be hurt but not her. Is that what you mean?"

"You're stronger, Penny. Stronger than Laura and stronger than Gerald."

"Much good that's done me!"

"You say you love Gerald. If you love him, you'll want to help him."

"I do love him, Ted. So much that I can't bear to stand by and watch him marry someone else."

"Love should not be selfish."

"Selfish! I'm not the selfish one. What about you? Why do you go on coming here, pleading for Gerald? Where do you fit into all this?"

"I need Gerald as much as he needs you."

Penny thought about that a lot after Ted had gone. Did Ted need Gerald emotionally or to further his career? On the answer to that hinged an explanation of Gerald's needing her.

If he was just a fortune-hunter, then he could not start his new business deal without her. If he really loved her, then he needed her support in the difficult role he must play. Only Gerald could tell her, but she could not trust herself to see him. The power of his attraction would sweep away all arguments. Remembering the ardour of her response to his kisses consumed her with humiliation. His hold over her had been so great that he must still believe she'd do anything for him. Even stay around to pick up the crumbs of love while he married someone else. She had put herself in an unbearable position. Pride upheld her decision never to see Gerald again.

It was pride that made her go to work each day and act as if nothing had happened. She had never worn an engagement ring and so nobody asked any questions. Once inside the flat on a Friday evening she gave way to the surge of misery. Food — even the thought of it — sickened her. Her only relief was in sleep and she fell into bed early, waiting for oblivion to engulf her. She didn't need to look in a mirror to know that her appearance matched her mood.

Waking one Saturday morning, she felt so terrible that she was forced to take a long hard look at herself. To the face in the mirror, she murmured, "Penny Plain! You look absolutely dreadful."

She decided to waive breakfast and take a shower. The sharp tingling of the fine spray of water against her flesh eased her out of the sleep she still hankered to hide in. It made her consider her appearance and so she shampooed her hair. She did so vigorously as if she could wash away all the memories and miseries of the past weeks. Just as she'd dried herself and wrapped a towel turban-wise round her head, the doorbell pealed. She was startled, afraid to answer it, yet unwilling to let her visitor go. It might be Gerald. There might be a way out of this nightmare yet. Hastily, she flung her arms into a towelling robe and flew to the door. She stared at it blindly, willing the bell to ring again. It did. Apprehensively, she called:

"Who is it?"

"Penny, it's me. Chris."

"Oh!"

Relief and disappointment engulfed her. She could have cheered in her lightheadedness that she hadn't to face another decision. Yet her whole being felt empty to discover that Gerald wasn't there after all.

"Penny?" Chris called urgently and she could hear him turning the door handle.

"I — It's locked," she offered unhelpfully, dithering between surprise and a growing sense of comfort that Chris had come.

"Unlock it then!" he shouted unceremoniously.

"I — I — I was taking a shower and washing my hair. I — I'm not dressed yet."

"I'll wait," he answered curtly, but she didn't go to get dressed. Instead, she opened the door and, as he moved in, threw herself at him, sobbing hysterically. She thought she heard him swear, but his arms, as he drew her to him, were gentle. She buried her face in his chest and felt his hands firm and warm on her back. All she wanted to do was stay in the haven of his arms and cry and cry until there were no tears left. All the pent-up feelings of the past weeks spilled out in hot, trembling tears. It was like coming home to rest there against him. When the outburst slowed then stopped at last, he lifted her chin until she was forced to meet his eyes, then chided "Hey, what's all this about, Penny?"

"I'm sorry," she murmured indistinctly, "I'm making such a fool of myself."

As if in agreement the heavy turban teetered, then fell from her head, leaving her wet hair to flick its damp tendrils over his shirt.

"I can see I need to protect myself," he laughed and, picking up the towel, proceeded to rub her hair vigorously. When it was done, he mopped her tear-stained face before throwing the towel carelessly on to a chair.

"There! You look quite angelic now with that halo of curls."

Penny ran her fingers through her hair, childishly parting the tangles that clung damply to her head.

"You'll never believe I'm grown up now," she managed shakily as she sniffed back the remaining tears.

"Dressed like that I might!" he teased, his expression softening as he took in her scantily clad body. Penny felt the colour run up into her cheeks, chasing away the pallor that had previously been unmasked.

"I — I'd better dress."

She backed hastily to her bedroom

door, hiding her confusion over the thick robe that had fallen apart in his embrace. Her fingers shook as she pulled on fresh underwear, a skirt and a big floppy top that concealed her figure completely.

"Ah," murmured Chris as she re-entered the lounge, "this is more the Penny I know. Penny Plain!"

"Just a child, I suppose." She accused him crossly, smarting at his use of the old nickname for her though she had thought it herself only this morning.

"You were acting like one just now," he countered drily.

"I take it that it wasn't all pleasure at seeing me?"

She swung round on him, her eyes flashing: "Did you imagine that any of those tears were for you, Christopher Lloyd! Why, you never could make me cry. Not even when we were children."

"No, Penny. You took a delight then in proving that nothing could hurt you."

He sounded wistfully proud of the

self-reliant little girl she had been. Looking at him, Penny had no idea how desolate and bewildered her eyes were. She desperately wanted to find the words that would bring his sympathy and understanding. All she could say was: "I must have been a conceited minx. I can't think why you bothered with me. I wasn't worth your time."

"I always was the better judge of that, Penny. Now, supposing you tell me what happened to that prickly pride of yours."

"What do you mean?"

"Don't pretend with me, Penny. Something has happened to flatten you. What is it?"

She wanted to tell him, wanted to pour out all her troubles and have him sort them out. Perhaps he could make Gerald see sense. He'd find a solution. He had always been good at righting wrongs. She started to tell him, to let the whole story tumble out, but the words stuck in her throat and the room spun dizzily around her. She felt his grip on her arms and then she was sitting down with her head forced none too gently between her knees. When she was allowed to lift her eyes she saw that his expression was serious and anxious.

"Stay still, Penny," he ordered and his hand on her shoulder made sure of that. His eyes raked her face mercilessly and then, in an infinitely gentle voice, he asked: "It's bad, isn't it, Penny love?"

She tried to answer but again the give-away tears welled up in her eyes and choked her voice.

"Don't say anything, yet. I'll make some coffee."

"Thank you."

"Did you have breakfast?"

"I — I couldn't."

"Then I'll have to make you. Stay there while I see what I can do."

Penny couldn't find enough strength in her legs to show him into her tiny kitchen. She supposed that he wouldn't find it too easy to poke around in any kitchen. After all, he was used to being waited on. She wondered idly why he had come here today and knew that really she should have been offering him coffee. What would he think of her London manners? Anyway, it didn't matter. Nothing mattered any more. When last she'd seen Chris she'd been Gerald's girl. The hurt welled up inside her again that Gerald had been with Laura all the time she'd been defending their love to Chris. "He loves me," she'd declared when Chris had questioned Gerald's motives. Now he could see for himself how deep that love had been. He hadn't yet said "I told you so!" Doubtless he would later.

But Chris said little at all as he pulled a low table up to the side of her chair and another to the sofa. When he returned again from the kitchen, he carried a tray with cups of steaming coffee. Silently he handed one to her and left his own on a table while he went back for breakfast. He had prepared each of them a tray with toast and fluffy golden scrambled egg. There was marmalade to follow and, surprised at her hunger, Penny devoted all her attention to the food on her plate. She had eaten the lot and had a second cup of coffee before Chris chose to speak. He leaned back, looking very much at home, and she was struck by the air of authority that flowed from him. He seemed so much older than her now, with an underlying strength and power that the years had given him.

"What have you been doing with yourself, Penny? Playing with fire?"

She nodded slightly, unable this time to defend herself. Chris was not usually a gentle person but, in spite of that latent hint of savagery, he could be. She knew that. Where his heart was involved he would protect. She wanted his protection now so the barrier of pride was broken and she began her story. It all poured from her as it had happened. Her love for Gerald. Their partnership in the hotel. His affair with Laura, the baby and the attempted suicide. She didn't spare herself in the telling. She had expected too much of Gerald, had built up their relationship into something rare and wonderful. What had hurt most was that, in the end, she'd had to accept that she and Gerald were strangers to each other's deepest feelings. To her it was impossible that he could contemplate marrying another girl when Penny loved him so much. She realised now that marriage didn't mean the same to Gerald as it did to her. He thought he was offering her love when he begged her to stay with him. She ought to be big enough to stand by him now and give him the support he needed. Blindly, she turned her head from Chris so that he wouldn't see the fresh tears forming in her eyes. Please God, he wouldn't be kind to her now or she'd make a fool of herself again.

To prevent his sympathy, she invited his criticism by railing against herself: "I'm not with it enough, Chris. I haven't got what it takes. I talk of love but for all that I've failed him."

Chris bent forward to touch her lightly on the shoulder. "My Penny. Do you remember how your father used to call you Penny Precious?"

"Yes, but it seems so long ago."

"Find yourself again, Penny. Find that precious valued person who was made to be loved."

"But Gerald loved me in his way."

"His way!" Chris spat at her. "And what kind of way was that? Haven't you learnt yet what kind of man he is? He's a parasite living on those gullible enough to let him. Gerald has nothing to give you, but he'd suck you dry in a matter of years."

"I think I'm beginning to understand him now."

"Then get out while you can."

"I think I should like to go on working with him. You see, the hotel is all I've got. Just because he's going to marry Laura doesn't mean that I can't claim my share of the business we've started together."

"Started? Penny is your money tied up in this hotel?"

"Yes."

"And he planned to marry you to gain control of the business?"

"No! He's going to marry Laura."

"You must let him buy you out at once."

"Neither of us can afford to buy the other out."

"He could leave you in possession."

"Why should he?"

"Why indeed! He has found the right girl to push him to success. She has drive. She'll build him up as being someone in his own right. If anyone can make him succeed it will be his Laura, not you. He'll fall back on you as the sweet alternative. Oh, yes! There'll be plenty of crumbs to pick up from Laura's table. But will you be content with crumbs, my Penny?"

"It needn't be like that! I must accept their marriage, but I can still go on working with Gerald."

"Oh, Penny! Do you honestly believe it will stop there?"

"Why not?"

"Because Gerald will understand that you are staying around because you still want to be his."

"I can't be now. That's what hurts so."

"And that's what you must accept."

Chris crossed to her chair and pulled her up gently against the tautness of his whole long strength.

"Growing up can hurt like hell, Penny, but you can avoid most of the pain if you act wisely."

"I'm as old as you!"

"So you keep saying and you almost make me forget how young you really are."

"If I have so much to learn, Chris, stay and teach me. Show me how to make Gerald want me and only me. Help me, Chris, please help me."

Gently he disengaged himself from her clinging arms and, as if he hadn't heard her plea, said: "Let's go to the zoo, Penny Plain."

"The zoo!"

"Yes. Pack up some bread and we'll buy nuts to feed the animals."

"Are you crazy, Chris? I ask for your help and all you want is to feed the animals at the zoo."

"You can forget your troubles when you're watching others live."

"I don't want to forget!"

"Maybe not. But I don't want to spend the rest of the day with a tearful child, so let's have a treat."

He began to pick up their trays and carry them out to the kitchen, calling back to her: "You have the time it takes me to wash this lot up to get ready. Hurry now!"

In spite of herself, Penny grinned and felt her heart growing lighter as she sped into her bedroom to apply a light cover of make-up to her pale face. A pretty honey-toned blusher gave her cheeks a brighter glow and her now dry hair fluffed around her face attractively. Penny didn't think the zoo warranted a change of dress so she was ready by the time Chris emerged from her kitchen carrying a small screwed-up bag of scraps. He held it out to her, his dark eyes narrowed with an expression it was hard to define.

"Bread for the ducks."

"Oh, Chris! Do you remember how we used to feed the ducks on the river at home?"

"Yes — and you were scared of the swans."

"Never!"

"Oh, yes, you were! But never mind. I'll hold your hand if there are swans at the zoo."

"Thanks!"

So they left in a flurry of laughter and it was a gaiety that didn't let up for the rest of the morning. Chris chuckled, his teeth white and strong in the lean, tanned face, when a big lumbering elephant they were watching executed some steps reminscent of a curtsy. Penny giggled at the monkeys and they both laughed outright at a giraffe conversing with a sparrow, its long neck bowed down to reach the tiny feathered visitor. They stayed a long time in the children's corner as if together they could recapture their own childhood. Penny felt safe here. It was one place in London where she had never been with Gerald so there were no memories to haunt her.

Occasionally, a stab of pain caught her unawares and she tried to locate it. It was only the pain of a sorrow whose immediacy had been removed. She needn't remember why it hurt her. All need for thought and decision had been removed. Here she was in a time and place suspended. Nothing had meaning. Only the moment. Penny took each moment as a gift and, with Chris, watched time chase it away.

When they were hungry, they agreed to find a place to eat. The café they discovered was small, clean and cheerful. Both of them chose plaice with peas and chips, then followed it with apple-pie and cream. Afterwards,

Penny ordered a chocolate ice-cream and giggled at Chris's expression of mock horror.

"I told you you were still a little girl."

"So you did!"

She could only agree with him in her present mood, but he had become suddenly serious. "There are some experiences it is better for a sweet young girl not to have had."

"Not to fall in love! Really, Chris!"

"People fall out of love too, Penny."

"Some people may, but not me."

As her face creased back into its look of hurt and misery, Chris shook off his solemn mood and tried again to cheer her up. It was obvious to him that today was not the time to try to make Penny see reason. She had to break free from her own feelings, had to see Gerald in his true colours for herself.

Throughout the afternoon he deliberately avoided any mention of Gerald, the hotel or Penny's feelings. He insisted on a trip to the British Museum, declaring that his education had been neglected in this respect. On the tube, Penny was convinced she saw Gerald. His sleek fair hair gleamed as he concentrated on the open newspaper that screened his face. Penny felt her heart beat faster as he rose to meet their train. He'd surely see her now. But no, it was a strange face that met her welcoming smile without recognition. He wasn't even as tall as Gerald and his shirt collar was frayed. How could she have made such a mistake? She turned back to Chris, who was watching her closely, and launched into a bright conversation that did nothing to deceive him. However, it diverted her thoughts and, applauding her courage, Chris did his utmost to keep her happy.

They were back in her flat, drinking coffee when Penny had the most fabulous idea. "Chris, have you got to go back tonight?"

"No, why?"

"Then stay here."

"Penny! What are you suggesting? My own reputation may be beyond repair, but there's yours to consider."

"Chris, nobody cares what I do now."

"Don't you care yourself?"

"I'm so desperate I don't know what I want."

"Well, you needn't try to seduce me to ease your broken heart. How could you, Penny? You're a fool to yourself. I've a damned good mind to take you back home."

The idea of going home with Chris appealed to her far more than she dared to admit. He seemed to have assumed some kind of responsibility for her. She looked at him, pleading for a sign of compassion, but a chilling anger narrowed his gaze. "If I took you home you'd only go on plaguing the life out of me. You'll have to sort this mess out for yourself."

"Yes, Chris. I'm sorry."

"You should be! Trying to flirt with me, indeed! I could slap you — "

"But you flatter yourself. I wasn't offering to share my bed, only to put you up."

"Indeed. And you thought I could be put up without taking advantage of the situation. I'm a normal man, you know!"

"I've never thought of you in that way."

"Then perhaps you should! I could soon make you forget friend Gerald if I chose. Going to risk it again, Penny?"

She turned on him then, angry at the picture of her he was making. "I'd never fall in love with you, so there's no risk."

"Oh!" His voice was deceptively low and he moved in on her relentlessly. Sparks glowed in his eyes as he moulded her against him and his lips, when they found hers, were demanding in their long, slow possession. Instinctively, she wound her arms round his neck, vitally aware of his maleness and, when he pulled away, she still clung to him. Lightly now, he kissed the top of her head and there was laughter in his voice when he said: "Penny Plain! You're a fraud! You are still the little girl who came to the big bad city. After that, how could I take your love affair seriously? Gerald didn't teach you a thing."

"I've had other boyfriends, you know!" Penny retorted, piqued that he should find her naivety amusing.

"Boys, yes," he agreed with her. "But I thought we were talking of a woman's heartbreak until I found you still unawakened."

"Just because I'm not easy game for you!"

"Sorry, little Penny. I forgot myself. I thought Gerald would have taught you more about life, but your lips still have the scent of primroses on them."

"And what does that mean?" she asked, her curiosity aroused by his strange remark so that her desire to remain aloof was overcome.

"You may think you are an experienced woman, little one, but your countryside innocence is still there."

"Innocence!" The word on Chris's lips made her feel shame at the way she had let Gerald make a fool of her. She'd practically forced a proposal out of him and he hadn't really wanted her, only her money. Now, with Chris, she began to despise herself almost more than she despised Gerald. By building up her innocence Chris had made her aware how she'd betrayed her true self. Yet, he hadn't finished with her.

"Yes, innocence, Penny. You are still as fresh and dewy-eyed as when you first left home."

"Don't, Chris! Please."

"You've got to be told. Someone has to teach you, though God forbid that it should be me! Penny, you were made to love completely, to give yourself without thought. Never again could your lips be cool once you'd tasted love. Don't waste your time with Gerald, my dear. Don't waste your tears on him. You need a man who'll take your heart, master your chaste soul and love you as you ought to be loved."

"Someone like you, Chris?" she tried to joke.

"I told you. God forbid!"

"All this because I asked you to stay on in London for the night?"

He looked at her penetratingly as she struggled to lighten the mood, then capitulated by saying: "As it happens I am staying overnight."

"Here?"

"Hardly! It wouldn't seem fair to wine and dine Joanna, then return here to bed!"

"Joanna!"

"Yes. You never asked why I was in town. Well, I came up to take Joanna to a party tonight. I must leave soon or I shan't have time to change for dinner."

So he hadn't come just to see her! She had originally asked him to stay on because she'd hoped to cook a meal for them both. But he was taking Joanna out to dinner. He'd done his duty by taking Penny to the zoo. Now he must feel he deserved the reward. He was standing ready to go. She must let him leave quietly. She wasn't so young that she'd make a fuss. He wasn't going to sort out her problems. He wasn't the big brother she'd thought him. She tried to smile politely as she walked with him to the door. "Goodbye, Chris. Have a nice evening."

"And you, Penny. Take yourself to bed and catch up on some of the sleep you've been missing."

"Yes. Sleep is a cure for all ills."

"Your cure lies with Mr. Limpeney, Penny. Get in touch with him and get him to sort out this business with Gerald."

"Gerald can't afford to lose my money."

"That's his problem! You get free of it."

"I can't. Mr. Limpeney isn't my solicitor any more. Gerald fixed me up with his man."

"Damn and blast, Penny! You leave it this late to tell me that!"

"It's all right, Chris. Gerald and I understand each other now.

"Do you? Is that why you've cried all day?"

"Well, I've got to do something. I may not get Gerald back, but the hotel is all I have."

"It needn't be. We must get you another solicitor. Look, I can't stop now, but I'll have somebody get in touch with you. Don't do anything until then."

"I'm going to keep an interest in that hotel, Chris, if it's the last thing I do."

"Good God, Penny! Haven't you learned a thing? Make a break now. A clean break."

"Will you help me, Chris?"

"I'll see that you get the right backing. After that, you're on your own."

"Oh!"

"How much does this hotel scheme

mean to you, Penny?"

"Everything. It's my life."

"Then make it a life worth living. Don't remain in partnership with a parasite."

"But — "

"No buts, Penny. Try to grow up. I'm off now. I hate leaving you in need of care and protection, but you must learn for yourself who to run to."

"Not to you obviously! You have Joanna."

"I shan't if I don't rush. Goodbye, Penny Plain. Take care!"

He bent and kissed the tip of her nose and then went out of the door, straightening his shoulders as though he were glad to go. Penny wondered why this should hurt her as much as it did.

5

AS it happened. Penny cooked dinner for Ted that evening. He arrived while she was still smarting over Chris's attitude. It had been so obvious that an evening with the sophisticated Joanna meant more to him than the problems of a girl he considered a nuisance. He'd said that she plagued the life out of him. Well, she didn't! She'd show him that she could stand on her own two feet. Never again would she ask his advice or throw herself on his mercy. She'd worked with Gerald before and she could go on working with him. Why give up her security because he was going to marry someone else? She would prove to Chris how grown up she could be, how realistic. The business was as much hers as Gerald's and she was still his partner.

She said as much to Ted when he arrived with his woebegone face as long and pale as ever.

"True," he agreed. "That's what Gerald has been trying to tell you."

"That he needs my money?"

"That he needs you as a friend and as a business partner. Even Laura agrees."

"Oh!"

"She wants to be friends too."

Penny wasn't taken in by that. She knew that Laura had assessed to the nearest penny what was in such a friendship for her. But, if she was prepared to make Penny's life easy, then why throw away the chance? All wasn't lost. She'd play this scene cool and invite Gerald and Laura round for a drink one evening next week. Then they could finalise the deal and get back to work on the hotel. Ted, when she told him over dinner, allowed himself one of his rare smiles that transformed the length of his face into a likeable gentleness.

"Good for you, Penny. I'm glad you made the decision."

"You'll be able to go your own way, too, Ted. No more go-between."

"That's true. It's been difficult to explain to June why I haven't had much free time lately."

"Is that the girl you met at our party?"

"Yes. In fact, I knew her before, but Gerald asked me to escort Laura that evening."

"You mean he invited Laura himself?"

"She insisted on coming and he could hardly have brought her himself."

"Well, quite a web of deceit!"

"I'm sorry, Penny, for my part in it, but I think it will be best for you in the end."

"Faithful Ted! Even now you can't bring yourself to say that I'll be well rid of Gerald."

"As a husband, he was never your type. You're too nice."

"Thank you."

"Would you like me to come and

121

give you moral support on the evening you have them round?"

The idea appealed to Penny and she felt expansive enough to add: "Bring June. I'd like to get to know her."

It would leave her the odd one out, but she wasn't prepared to pretend an interest in another man just for the sake of appearances. They must know very well what they'd done to her and she wouldn't play their game of easy come easy go.

Chris phoned the same evening that she was entertaining Gerald and Laura. Excusing herself she took the call in her bedroom. Chris explained that he'd found the very man to deal with Penny's financial interest in the hotel. There was no need for her even to see Gerald again and she'd have her own money to buy herself into a more suitable arrangement. This solicitor would go so far as to advise her on her next move so that she could be assured of a secure future. He'd organised it all. Sewn up her whole life into a nice tidy packet!

Feeling the anger beginning to rise at his high-handed manner, Penny took pleasure in telling him softly: "Thank you, Chris, but you're too late."

"What do you mean?"

There was a dangerous edge to the voice on the phone so that Penny was glad she could rub in her independence without facing her adversary.

"I've already signed an agreement with Gerald. I'm staying in business with him."

"Hell, Penny! Are you crazy?"

"No, quite sane, Chris. Thank you for bothering, but I told you I'd sort it out."

"I'm coming over now."

"Oh! Are you in London again? What are you doing this time?"

"Playing nursemaid to you! Stay where you are until I get there. And pray I don't wring your silly little neck."

"Chris! Hang on! You can't come here now."

There was a long pause then a harder voice asked quietly: "Why not?"

"Because I'm not alone."

Like a whiplash came two words, clipped and clear: "Who's there?"

"S-s-some friends."

"Who?"

There was no fobbing him off with half-truths. Well, he'd asked for it: "Gerald."

"He's there now, in your flat?"

"Yes."

"Goodbye, Penny."

"But, Chris — " She stared into the receiver, knowing that he couldn't hear her. He'd slammed down the phone before she could explain. His farewell had been a sneer, his voice registering contempt. Would he come as he'd threatened? She spent the rest of the evening less bothered about her reaction to Gerald and Laura than about Chris's arrival. She dreaded the ring of her doorbell, yet after she had shown out her guests and tidied up she gave way to the disappointment she felt that Chris had stayed away. Where was he, she wondered, and what must he think of her now? It was strange how much his good opinion of her mattered when it was Gerald she loved.

Despite an over-cordial invitation from Laura to the wedding, Penny left London the Friday before the ceremony. It had been arranged between her and Gerald that she move into Avon House and sort out some of its teething problems before they officially opened. Although some of their staff were already appointed, it would be necessary to hire more locally. Some of the residential staff would be moving in too, so there was plenty for Penny to sort out. She and Gerald had discussed the problems at length, so she knew exactly what to do. Once again she had been impressed by the way they worked together. Their ideas complemented one another and they would make a good team. In fact, Gerald gave her more say as a partner than he had ever done as a prospective wife. Together, they could not fail to make a success of the business.

Penny drove down to Devon in the small van they'd bought for the hotel. It was a long and tiring drive and she was glad when she first sighted the name of Lyttery on a signpost. At last she was within reach of the village near Avon House. She would stop there and have some tea just in case there was nothing at the hotel. The village, as she entered it, was bathed in the mellow light of an autumn afternoon.

In some ways it reminded Penny of home and she felt sadness rise up inside of her. If only she had been going home where love and comfort always waited for her. She had never felt so completely alone in her whole life. Such beauty shone all around her and the outlying countryside spoke of peace and gentle growth, yet for her there was only loneliness. Her hands tightened involuntarily on the wheel and she had to fight an uncontrollable urge to drive straight on, leaving Lyttery and

Avon House asleep in the afternoon sunshine. Perhaps it was for others and not for her to awaken the peace of the little village. She could drive on into the sunset until she'd left every reminder of her earlier life behind. How fanciful! A cup of tea should restore her senses. She found a parking place and clambered out of the van. It wasn't ideal for long distances. A brisk walk along the village street should restore her circulation. She must make a point of getting to know people here, they'd be real people, deep and reliable like those she'd known as a child.

Tea over, Penny drove on — through the long village street with its shops on either side then left over a little humped bridge. It was so narrow that she had to wait to let an oncoming car pass first. She could see a swan moving gracefully on the water and a host of ducks darting out beaks for bread at the water's edge. Children were feeding them and laughing at their antics. How often she had done the same, imagining the swans as monstrous water dragons and Chris as the knight to save her. After the bridge, the road meandered on, following a small stream, until a left-hand fork revealed a long gravel drive and the house beneath it. It didn't nestle in the fold of the hill as old country houses are said to do, but stood starkly simple against the green of rising fields. It was uncluttered and impressive. Penny admired Gerry's genius in finding it. Here, the cool of country freshness would enhance the new cool of sophisticated life. It was ideally situated for the kind of clientele they anticipated.

Later, inside, Penny found that Gerald had echoed the stark simplicity in the decor. Gone was the little cubby-hole of reception she'd first seen when they'd viewed the place. In its stead was a wide, spacious area out of which the staircase spiralled upwards. Penny was gazing at it entranced when Ted appeared at her elbow.

"Hello, Penny. June's getting a room ready for you for tonight."

"Ted! You're here already. How nice!"

Ted was to be their barman and Penny had promised to school June for reception. It was obvious she'd be an asset if she was already helping out with room service. Penny found her in a large bed-sitting-room in the wing reserved for staff. Shyly, she explained: "I chose this room for you because I think it is the nicest but perhaps you'd prefer something different?"

Penny remembered the flatlet she and Gerald had picked out for their own. It would be his and Laura's now. As a partner, she supposed she could insist on a flat too, but this room was large and comfortable.

"This will do perfectly, thank you."

"Ted thought you would like the view," June added and crossed to a large expanse of window down one side of the room. Fields opened out as if an extension to the room itself and, high above, clumps of woodland screened the sky.

"How lovely!" Penny exclaimed. "When I was little, we used to have a painting just like that and I often wished that I could walk into it. Now I have my own landscape and I can go out into it as well."

"Don't forget the stairs!" Ted quipped, coming in with her cases. He looked so much more relaxed down here and was actually smiling at his own joke. Penny was touched by the care the two had taken to choose her a room well away from the flatlet, yet one that had a natural personality to suit her. She couldn't wait to go over the rest of the house and see the results of careful planning. There was still much to do but Avon House was beginning to breathe with a separate life of its own. When she climbed into bed much later that night Penny felt that she could sleep for a week. It was not the sleep of escape she'd sought ever since Laura's attempted suicide, but gentle, satisfying relaxation after an exhausting day. Someone had switched on an electric blanket and the bed was beautifully warm and comfortable. She put out the light and snuggled down, for the first time in months actually looking forward to the day to come.

Gerald and Laura were honeymooning in Austria for a week so Penny was alone in command. Already, local people used the bar in the evenings so Ted was busy. June coped with the arriving staff Gerald had hired in London and Penny advertised locally for room-maids and waitresses. They needed more kitchen staff too, especially as they had no chef to date. Gerald hadn't found any of the applicants up to his standard, so they were starting with none. Penny doubted that she'd find anything more than a plain cook locally, but knew that she could always cope herself if necessary. Luckily her training had been thorough, so she was ready to deal with all kinds of situations. She had never interviewed would-be employees before, though. She had to summon all her age and height to lend her authority for the occasion but still felt a tiny youngster before the middle-aged countrywomen who came. Some came out of curiosity and were quickly dispatched again. Others needed the work that a new place in their district might create. Penny searched for those who had an interest in the kind of work the hotel had to offer. She was pleased with the appointments she made, confident that they had enough to start the wheels turning.

She was especially pleased to take on three girls. She hadn't expected many applicants for the posts as waitresses when she'd advertised. Avon House was far enough out of the village to make living-in a necessity and there'd be evening work involved. Most country girls who stayed in their native villages did so because they preferred to live at home. The majority did what Penny had done herself and sought out the big cities. Penny found exceptions in Rosa and Jean. They were cousins but not in the least alike. Rosa was small and dark with mischief dancing in her brown eyes whereas Jean was tall and fair with a smile that was more watchful than warm. Each appealed to Penny in her own way and she took them to meet Charles. He was the head waiter Gerald had hired and, like most of his appointments, had worked with Gerald before. He was already trying to assert his authority over the skeleton kitchen staff they had and was not particularly inclined to regard Penny as the boss. He visibly puffed with pride on being consulted about the girls and subjected them to more questions than Penny had thought necessary for their interview. However, he couldn't fault their eagerness to learn and eventually declared himself satisfied. Penny detected the gleam in Rosa's eye that suggested she was a good little actress and knew it. She'd need watching! Far the most interesting find Penny had was in an older girl called Julie. She had come in answer to the advertisement for waitresses, but was quick to point out that she was really interested in learning all aspects of hotel work. Skilful questioning and genuine interest soon deduced that she'd started on the same training as Penny a few years ago. Then her father had died leaving an invalid widow and Julie had returned home. She hadn't had to nurse her mother. They could afford professional help, but Julie had never been able to go back to London. Her mother had depended on her completely until this summer. She'd died of a heart attack while Julie had been taking a holiday in France.

"The doctor made me go." She insisted to Penny as if to apologise for the break in the picture of a devoted daughter. Julie hadn't been able to face her new independence until she'd heard of the changes taking place at Avon House. Straight away, she'd known that it would be ideal for her. Here was a chance to gain practical experience in the field she'd once chosen for training.

"Mr. Hart said his wife might help me if I came back later."

"You've met Mr. Hart?"

"Oh, yes. He came down several weekends. We had a drink together in the village."

"And he promised you a job?"

"Not exactly. He said that his wife had finished her training in management and might take me on as an assistant for a couple of years."

"You don't see this as a permanent post?"

"Not really. Just to get my confidence back. I expect to go into business on my own later."

"The same business?"

"Something smaller, perhaps. Gerald — that is Mr. Hart — said to be sure to ask to see him if I came."

"I'm afraid he isn't here at the moment, but I'm sure he meant you to work with me."

"Are you his wife?"

Penny tightened her stomach muscles, determined not to feel any hurt at these words.

"I am Gerald's business partner," she said quietly. "It was me he was going to marry, but he married someone else instead."

The other girl looked embarrassed and mumbled an apology. To put her at her ease Penny explained: "It's I who had the training in hotel management, so we'd be the ones who would be working together, you and I."

"And his wife?"

"She's not in the business," Penny answered idly, wondering why the girl should show an interest in Laura. She wasn't the type to appeal to the new Mrs. Hart anyway. Beneath the seemingly assured manner was a shyness Laura would find too amusing. This young woman still had the quiet of the country in her. She reminded Penny of herself when she'd first left home. Older of course, but, nevertheless, unspoilt. Her long, almost-fair hair was drawn back into a circlet at the back of her neck. Not fashionable, but it suited the nice open face it framed.

It was Julie who later helped Penny prepare the flat for the return of the newly-weds. June had offered to save Penny the embarrassment, but this was a situation that had to be faced. She went about the task as if preparing for strangers until Julie asked: "Can't we make it look more like home?"

"Home?"

"Well, it will be their home, won't it? At the moment it's little different from the guest rooms except in size."

"It was how Gerald wanted it. He said it could be given personality later."

"Was? Did you two choose this flat together? Before he married someone else?"

"Yes."

"But how can you bear to get it ready for them now?"

"It has to be done."

"Yes, but — "

"No buts. There's work to do. When we've finished here, there's a special meal to cook for this evening."

As it happened, they had scarcely finished and were taking a last look round when Laura burst in followed by Gerald. He seemed ruffled and concerned in a way Penny had never seen him. Laura, on the other hand, was cold and beautiful. She ignored the two girls in the room and went straight through to the bedroom. Penny noticed that she looked white and shaking and that she only just managed to reach the bed. She went in to her, but Laura only stared at the ceiling. Her body seemed slight in spite of its length along the bed. Penny felt sympathy well up in her as she asked:

"Aren't you feeling well?"

"My dear child, do I look it?"

"You look ill. Shall I call a doctor?"

"No, it'll pass. It'd bloody well better or I won't go through with this business."

"I don't understand."

"Oh, Christ! Miss Innocence! It's the baby, of course, cutting up rough. Didn't like the crossing."

"Oh!"

"Stop staring at me and do something."

"Yes, of course. How can I help you?"

"Go away!" screamed Laura, and Penny went helplessly back to the other room where Gerald and Julie were standing close together by the window. Gerald came straight over to Penny and took both her hands.

"Hello, Penny. Good to see you again." He leaned forward and kissed her brow, but she shrugged him off to ask: "But Laura? What can we do for her?"

"Leave her. She'll be all right soon. It was a hell of a journey." He spoke quite matter of factly as if used by now to Laura's outbursts.

"I'm going to have a rest myself for an hour. Julie here is going to bring up a tray."

So that was all they had been talking about! Penny went down to the kitchens feeling sorry for the newly-weds. Laura looked so worn out with pregnancy already and Gerald had to weather all her storms. It was Julie, preparing the tea-tray, who voiced her feelings: "Poor thing! Fancy having to put up with her!"

Penny surprised herself by thinking that he'd made his own bed. She lifted her chin. Let him lie in it!

After that first angry outburst Laura did nothing to cross Penny. She never put in an appearance until after lunch, taking the first two meals of the day with Gerald in their flat. How she spent her afternoons Penny never discovered, but she went off in her own Mini and usually returned some time after tea had been served. She rested until dinnertime, then came down looking elegant to share a table with Gerald, Penny, Ted and June. She was always the centre of attention and often Penny caught Rosa mimicking her dramatic gestures so exactly that even Charles was forced to turn aside to smile. He always supervised the serving of their dinner as meticulously as, half an hour later, he would start to hover over the other diners. Residents, of course, had reserved tables, but there was also quite a trade in evening meals for non-residents. Avon House was quickly establishing itself as the place to be seen locally and every man brought his wife or his mistress to sample its fare.

Penny often missed the formal gathering for dinner because she was busy in the kitchen. Her success as chef was such that Gerald was in no hurry to replace her although it added too much to her responsibilities. Julie helped her and, together, the two girls worked like clockwork. Their routine was well established one evening when June came into the kitchen from her post at reception.

"Can you manage two more, Penny?"

"We finished serving half an hour ago, June!"

"I know but I've a feeling these two are special."

"Why?"

"They said they've been recommended and stopped specially on their way back to London."

"O.K. We'll cope."

"Is anything off?"

"No, but they may have to wait a while for some dishes. Get them to order first, then spend half an hour in the bar."

"Right. Thanks."

With little more than a conspiratorial smile, Penny and Julie donned their aprons once again.

The order was by no means simple and Penny worked flat out for the next three-quarters of an hour. Then, assured that Julie could cope, she sank into the nearest chair with a cup of coffee. She was exhausted. Gerald would have to do something about this. She was reluctant to take her rest by leaving more of the business side to him. He had lost her trust. Now she considered it necessary to keep an ear to the ground and an eye on all things. She felt that Gerald would like to keep her in the kitchen more so that he could run things his own way.

She was lost in such thoughts when Gerald himself came into the kitchen. Unusual for him. His eyes searched the room until they alighted on Penny. He crossed to her. "Well done, Penny! We've scored there."

"Who is it? Royalty?"

"No," he laughed. "But influential. He's our youngest and most promising would-be tycoon. A dynamo, they say. And she'll get us some good publicity with her magazine."

"That's good. A lucky break."

"Now they want to meet the chef, so come along."

"No, Gerald," Penny demurred. "I've told you I'd have none of that."

"Just for once, Penny," Gerald pleaded.

"No. I'm off duty now and I intend to go up to my room."

Gerald didn't try again to get her to change her mind, but he asked: "Will you come down for a drink later?"

"Yes, of course. Everything as usual."

"Right." He was away looking very pleased with himself, considering.

Penny usually allowed herself an hour to relax from supervising the cooking and to take a bath and dress for her appearance in reception or the bar. Tonight was no exception. She had just stepped out of the bath when her phone rang. It was June. "Ted said I must tell you to look your best."

"Why?"

"I've no idea. Except that the couple they're making such a fuss about is still here. They're in the bar."

"Oh. And Ted gave you the message?"

"Yes. He said it was important."

"Well, I'll try to oblige. Thanks June."

She padded back to the bathroom to finish drying herself, then crossed to her wardrobe to select a dress. She'd lost weight lately and her slim figure needed elegance to lend it height. Otherwise she became a slip of a girl. She chose a long white dress with a high stand-away neckline that transformed a deceptively simple model. Her hair, which she had been growing, swept up away from the collar, leaving her face framed rather like an Elizabethan lady's might have been. The effect was sensational and June gasped as Penny swept down the grand staircase to reception. Coming from the kitchen, Julie stopped to admire. It was funny that, as Penny had adopted the more severe hairstyle, Julie was now crowned with a mass of fair curls. Just Gerald's taste.

In the bar Gerald came forward as she entered.

"Penny, how lovely! Do come and meet our guests."

He ushered her towards the small group in the corner.

"Now, at last, meet our chef!"

Even before they turned, Penny knew why Ted had sent the message. She had just cooked dinner for Chris and his Joanna! Her composure was perfect as Joanna purred: "You! Why, darling, how clever you must be!"

"Thank you." Penny accepted the compliment, waiting for Chris to speak. Well-cut dark trousers emphasised his height as he lounged against the bar, and a brown silk shirt deepened the tawny lights in his eyes. He was a man to be reckoned with in any sphere and handsome in a rugged fashion. His whole attitude was one of ease, yet there was an ever-present suggestion of tension as he bent his gaze to Penny.

"Chef? I thought you were supposed to be a partner."

Gerald looked more put out than Penny, his sensitive face paled and he stammered a bit trying to explain about their efforts to get a good chef. Penny knew that Chris would have been as competent in this field as Gerald had been unlucky. It occurred to her that he would be competent in anything he undertook.

Loyalty to Gerald made her shrug

and say: "I enjoy cooking so why not?"

"Why not indeed if you're happy," he returned and, later, to Penny alone, he repeated: "Are you happy, Penny? Really happy?"

His eyes demanded a truthful answer so Penny hedged by replying, "I like my work and there's plenty to do."

Chris looked at her carefully, not missing the fine sweep of her bones now that her face had lost its roundness.

"You're not working too hard, are you?"

"Impossible!"

"Will you be home for Christmas?"

His voice was low and she thought she sensed a note of entreaty in it. Her own defence was sure enough.

"We're holding a house-party here."

Joanna heard that and, quick to break into the téte-à-téte which had excluded her, exclaimed, "A Christmas houseparty! What fun!"

"Yes," Gerald enthused and went on to describe the kind of Christmas he had in mind. Joanna laid a slim hand on Chris's arm and asked, "Couldn't we come, darling?"

He seemed annoyed about something and answered sharply, "I can't. That's for sure."

Soon after he was the one who insisted that they must be leaving and his farewells were general. There was no special word for Penny, who watched him leave with Joanna, her dark head glossy against the breadth of his shoulder, and couldn't understand the strange new ache in her heart.

6

AS the weeks went by. Avon House hummed with an activity that gradually gave way to a buzz of expectation. Bit by bit, the elegant house was prepared for Christmas, and excitement seemed to thicken in the air as the final touches were made. Spring flowers, specially imported, took the place of conventional Christmas decorations, though the stark simplicity of reception was relieved by one silver tree stretching up in competition with the spiral staircase. Its shape had been designed to create this impression so its silver branches echoed the swirl of the stairs. Thus, a striking entrance to the hotel was established as well as being a beautiful background for the ladies who would decorate that staircase over Christmas.

Outside, hundreds of lights had been fitted up. The few trees which marked the entrance were strung with tiny coloured lights that, at night, twinkled in the shapes of cardboard cut-out Christmas trees. Floodlights bleached the already white walls of Avon House and picked out the welcoming wreath of tinsel and coloured lights that glowed on the front door. No expense was spared and nothing overlooked to make this first Christmas at Avon House memorable. The hotel was fully booked for the festive weekend so that the Friday before Christmas Eve saw everything ready, the scene set for success. A heady scent filled the air, perfuming everything with expectancy, but Penny did not recognise in it the magic of Christmas at home. Even when, next day, the first arrivals let in little flurries of snow and occasional flakes sparkled on dark furs before melting in the warmth of the house, she couldn't recapture the excitement of other Christmas Eves. She was too busy to ponder just what was missing as she contributed all her energies to provide everything any guest could want at Christmas. Gerald was determined that this house-party should go with a swing and there was an element of feverishness in all the efforts towards this end. Coming down to the fancy dress ball he had organised for the evening, Penny caught sight of Gerald and was reminded of a redcoat at a holiday camp. She laughed to herself at such a mental picture of him. Only a few months ago it would have shocked her. Had he really changed so much? From her secluded corner she watched him dance with a blonde girl with heavily made up eyes and a bored mouth. They danced very close together and Penny noticed the glances that moved in their direction. Laura chose to ignore them and, magnificent in dramatic black that made her skin glow like pearl, held court at one end of the ballroom. She was watching everyone, of course, from within the centre of her group of admirers. Her eyes caught Penny's gaze and, for a moment, the hostility was obvious until Laura smiled and waved an acknowledgement. Still so hostile? She'd won the man, hadn't she? Why should she resent Penny so? Why not glare at the blonde who clung so possessively to Gerald's arm even as the music stopped and people drifted to the tables at the sides of the ballroom? Suddenly, Penny disliked the atmosphere of false gaiety and would have left quietly had not Ted discovered her.

"So here you are! Why are you hiding away instead of dancing?"

"Because nobody asked me."

"You shouldn't have come down so late. June and I have been watching for you."

"Where's June now?"

"Dancing with the big boss man. He seems to be circulating well."

At that moment, Gerald swirled June round in front of them and, from the look in his eyes, Penny saw that he'd been looking for her. With scant ceremony, he handed June over to Ted and swept Penny away with a quick turn in time to the music.

"Will you dance, Penny?"

"Why not?"

"Why not indeed!" His voice whispered at her ear. "It's been an age, my lovely."

"What has, Gerald?" He could not have failed to notice the ice creeping into her voice.

"Waiting to hold you in my arms."

"Now look . . ." She tried to protest but his arms tightened as he said with feeling:

"I've done more than my fair share tonight. I've danced with every wife and girlfriend in the place."

"Then please don't bother about me."

"Don't be a fool!"

They were dancing at the edge of the room, near the french windows and, before Penny knew what he was about, they were out of the ballroom and on the little verandah that surrounded it. Gerald's arms were about her.

"And now . . . " he breathed. She had not been expecting the passionate embrace and the kisses that stirred forgotten depths. At first, shaken, she let him kiss her but too soon came that moment of surrender or fight. Penny fought. She struggled to free herself from his arms.

When, at length, he let her go and spoke, his voice was slurred and unsteady. "So now you know, Penny. I want you. I need you, by God I do!"

"Gerald, stop! All that is over between us."

"Never, Penny! I want you now more than ever."

"But Laura?"

"Laura's got what she wants. Now, I'm going to have my fun."

He made to pull her into his arms again, but Penny resisted and, holding aloof, said, "But not with me, Gerald. I'm not prepared to settle for what you now have to give."

Silence met such a refusal. Then, recovering, Gerald said, "You kept your claws well sheathed, little Penny. I never expected such a remark from you."

"Now you know."

"Ah, but I haven't given up yet. Only for tonight."

"Give up then for good. I'll never be anything to you now."

"Kiss me, Penny, then see if you can say that again."

Determined not to be provoked, Penny turned back into the ballroom to be swallowed up in the sea of dancers. A general 'Excuse Me' was in progress and she found herself swept on to the floor again and again as she sought to escape. At last the music stopped and, aware again of Laura's watchful eye, Penny saw with dismay the muddied hem of her costume dress. Snow had turned to slush on the verandah and her excursion outside with Gerald had left its mark. The dress had been hired so she must deal with the stains at once.

Murmuring her excuses, she hurried up to her room. There, she dealt with the offending frills then changed into a warm trouser suit for outdoors. She knew one of the things that was missing and there was a remedy for it.

She took the van and drove carefully up the long sweep to the road, the gravel crunching beneath the tyres. Once out on the road, she relaxed and allowed herself to become part of the starlit serenity. The night was bright with stars and their reflected light in the powdering of snow that brushed the fields. Even before she entered the little church in the village, Penny began to feel that peace which was always part of Christmas. She was in good time for the midnight service so she knelt quietly alone and let the peace steal over her. Home or here in this other village, it didn't matter. At the hotel she'd mistaken gaiety for joy. Truth lay inside her wherever she might be. Now the truth broke in her heart like a light. All over again, she understood the birth of the baby at Christmas, the true light which has lit the world for centuries. He had to be born in her and, in the service that followed, she committed herself to such a birth. This was as it had been every Christmas. This was as it must be. Penny, precious to herself, must be true to her own light.

Wrapped in this spirit of other worldliness, Penny returned to Avon House and smiled at the sounds of merrymaking from the ballroom. Tomorrow she would join in again but tonight was her own Christmas. In her room, she took out the parcels she'd received from home and opened them one by one. A book of her father's, slim and newly published, made her realise how much she'd lost touch. A fine stole, white with a silver thread, spoke of her mother's delicate handwork and loving care. What messages had her own hastily purchased gifts conveyed? The last parcel she opened was from Chris. Packed with her family's presents to her, she had not expected it to be from him though they'd always exchanged gifts. This one was small but heavy. Inside the holly-covered paper was a mass of white tissue and then the smooth round glass of her grandmother's favourite paperweight. It gleamed like crystal but beneath the surface, deep in its heart, were little bubbles of mother-of-pearl coloured light. Each bubble radiated delicate colour yet, at the surface, was still and clear. Always, this had fascinated her. How often she had held it to the light, exclaiming on its beauty to Chris and her grandmother. And Chris had bought it for her, rescued it from the sale. How like him! Feverishly, she searched among the tossed aside tissue paper for a message, but there was none. Only his name on the greetings card. She sat for a long time holding the smooth oval of glass in her hands. Only the thought of the work to be done the next day at last sent her to bed.

Christmas rushed into the New Year

and another weekend party, different only because they'd changed guests. Gerald was in his element but Laura began to look tired and rather pale. Nobody was surprised when, after all the decorations had been taken away and the hotel returned to normal, she announced her intention of spending a weekend with her mother. On the Friday morning Gerald drove her to the station then returned so full of high spirits that Penny did not need the signal from Ted's raised eyebrows to warn her that Gerald meant to enjoy his freedom. Nevertheless, when he invited her into the village for a shopping trip and tea, there didn't seem any harm in accepting.

It was a gay trip. Even the usual bulk purchases for the hotel, undertaken by an enterprising young man in a new store, took on a light-hearted note. They had finished in half the expected time so Gerald suggested a run in the car before tea. He had bought himself a new car, as long, low and sleek as the one he'd had in London, but, at Laura's insistence, it wasn't a convertible. Certainly, they were glad of its rich upholstery and cosy warmth this January afternoon. The sun shone through the windows, giving an illusion of spring since the bitter cold of the wind could not touch them. It was one of those days every January produces at least once with a promise of light and warmth to come. The car consumed the miles of undulating road without effort, and the changing scenery charmed Penny into a soft and happy mood. Some of the lanes were narrow and steep-sided, then opened out into broad sweeps of moorland. Penny had not realised they'd travelled so far when Gerald pulled on to a grass verge at the top of one hill and said:

"Now look!"

Below them, wild and beautiful, was the sea. It beat back against the pebbled beach, throwing up a white spray.

"How lovely!" exclaimed Penny.

"Oh, Gerald! Thank you."

"Glad you came?" he asked casually, and Penny's bright eyes gave him his answer.

"Would you like to go down?" he asked and to Penny's breathless "Can we?" he drew the car out on to the road again. Slowly they edged over the crest. It was steep and narrow, but to Penny that added to the excitement of coming down to the sea in winter. She didn't speak as the car nosed its way down, but as soon as they'd stopped she was out and running across the beach. Laughing, Gerald joined her, grabbing her hand to steady her as she lurched on the shifting stones. They were alone in the world and she gasped at the emptiness and coldness of the beach. Together, they ran to a little beach hut which proclaimed Teas in bright paint, but it was deserted and boarded up. In summer, this would be an ideal spot but now they were glad to clamber back to the car. They were still laughing at the shock of the cold and the dampness of the icy spray.

"Let's find somewhere for tea," suggested Gerald, and Penny was happy to agree. This was the easy-going, caring Gerald of the early days and she enjoyed having him back again. He fitted her mood as he'd always done and cared for her comfort. They enjoyed tea in companionable silence in a little village café not far from the beach, then they both knew that they must be back at Avon House for the evening meal. Penny sensed Gerald's reluctance to return but she didn't realise how much he'd misjudged her feelings that afternoon. He'd thought her acquiescence a prelude to greater pleasure as he was to prove later that night.

Dinner with Ted and June was gay. Gerald motioned Charles to bring the wine list and chose a sturdy, robust accompaniment to their roast hare, quite unlike the light-bodied everyday drinking wine that they usually shared. Julie was cooking and, as there were few guests, she'd gone to town on the young hare that one of the bar customers had brought in. Without Laura at the table, there was an air of freedom and they all lingered over their coffee, enjoying the relaxed atmosphere. The few residents still with them cast amused glances at their laughter as they settled to enjoy their own meals. Now Gerald excused himself from the table and became the genial host. Ted made his way to the bar and June and Penny wandered into reception aware that there was going to be time for conversation and relaxation that evening. It was after she'd seen how little Ted had to cope with in the bar and had checked the scrubbed and empty kitchen awaiting the morning staff that Penny went up to her own room. As she came along the corridor she could see that a light was on inside. Funny! She was sure she'd turned off that light before going down to dinner. She opened the door slowly, not sure what to expect, and there was Gerald sprawled out in her easy chair with an ice bucket holding champagne at his side. As she went in, he sprang up to greet her:

"I've brought a drink to celebrate, darling."

"Celebrate what?"

"Us, being together again."

"But Gerald — "

"Come now, Penny, no buts. You enjoyed our drive this afternoon, didn't you?"

"Yes, of course."

"And we were together."

"Yes."

"Then let's be happy about it. Once you were pleased to drink to a successful partnership and now we've got it."

Penny remembered the occasion he referred to, before the party that brought Laura into her life. She'd been so happy then, only too pleased to dance and drink with Gerald. His voice now, as he held out her glass, was as low and attractive as ever.

"To us, Penny?"

She couldn't refuse to drink with him; he looked so charmingly boyish. She laughed at his insistence and said, "To the hotel and all who work in it."

It was like old times to be alone with him and, under the influence of the champagne, she began to relax. She kicked off her shoes and subsided into the chair he'd vacated. He didn't go to another. Dangerously close, he reclined on the arm of the chair she sat in. His arm brushed her shoulder. He looked down on her and a teasing laughter broke across his face. This was Gerald as Penny remembered him, her Gerald. She could not move though her body seemed to want to melt towards him and her spirit drew back in shame. She wondered if he was going to kiss her and, if so, what she would do. His face seemed to come nearer without moving.

"Penny, my darling!"

His voice was full of pleasure, the pleasure she, too, felt at his closeness.

Then, suddenly, his full weight was upon her as they plunged into the kiss. It took her a long time to understand. At first, the nestling warmth of the embrace and his hands curving round the softness of her breasts were full of the familiarity of past caresses. Then the sound deep in his throat, as his fingers bit in and hurt her, startled her into full awareness. Her dress tore as his hands dragged at her and his mouth insistently sucked her towards him as he found even more of her naked flesh to fondle. His body, hard and spiky, seemed to crush her and every part of her wanted to reject its demanding manhood. She struggled to free herself, fear now joining the repulsion that filled her. Fear and shame gave her the strength to roll out from under him and to reach the emptiness of the floor.

"What's the matter?" His hands still stretched out to take her, so she rolled farther away.

"Penny, whatever's the matter?"

Pulling herself to her feet, still shaking yet trying to tidy her dress about her, Penny said, "I'm sorry, Gerald. I'm sorry."

"What do you mean?"

His eyes were narrow and watching her but even he seemed genuinely affected by the depth of feeling in her voice.

"I'm sorry, Gerald. I must have led you to think this could be. But it can't. Not ever. I know now that you and I are wrong. We always were wrong together, but I didn't know it then."

"You didn't think we were wrong together this afternoon."

"But it should have stopped at that."

"Oh, for God's sake, Penny! Right or wrong! Should and shouldn't! What matters is that it'll be all right. Is that what's worrying you? It'll be all right, I'm telling you."

"Go away, Gerald. And never come near me again."

She was immensely sad and tired but even he could see that she was in command of the situation. He took refuge in mockery.

"Quite the princess! Well, go back to your ivory tower. Not good enough for you, is that it?"

"This is something to do with myself, Gerald, being true to myself."

His eyes were angry and his voice spiteful as he flung at her: "Yourself! That's all you're likely to have, you frigid little bitch."

Penny could say no more. He banged out of the room, gone, she knew, for ever. She didn't even bother to lock the door before she pulled off the torn gown, then went into her tiny bathroom to drown the feel of him in the sharp, stinging water of the shower.

Penny couldn't settle to the empty room even after she'd scrubbed herself clean and changed all her clothes. She wanted to go and talk to Ted and June, nice, comforting Ted whose loyalty to Gerald had once annoyed her. Now she knew it as the loyalty of someone paid for his services. Ted had a different kind of loyalty to Penny, one rooted in affection. He and June would make the world turn normally again. But, to talk to them, she'd have to go down to the bar. Gerald might have gone there too. She wasn't afraid to meet Gerald but she preferred to stay out of his way until her decision was made. She'd go and talk it over with Julie. They weren't exactly soul mates but they'd worked together a lot lately. Julie was cool and her advice would be considered.

A sound caught Penny's ear even as she knocked at Julie's door, a furtive stir of sound like the soft laugh of a man at pleasure. She recognised the drift of amusement before the door opened, but she could not turn away. She stood still. Julie opened the door just a fraction. She looked flushed and confused to see Penny standing there.

"Oh, it's you!" she stammered as she drew her short, quilted housecoat around her. It was as obvious that she had nothing on beneath it as it was that there was someone else in the room. Penny only wanted to get away.

"Sorry, Julie! I didn't think you'd be in bed."

"I — I had a bit of a headache. Is it important?"

"Not at all. It was only about that new shellfish recipe. We'll talk about it tomorrow. Goodnight, Julie."

Anything to get away quickly. But she wasn't quick enough. Gerald knew it was her and he knew that she had guessed who was in the room. Now he made certain.

"For God's sake, hurry!" he called to Julie and there was no mistaking his tone. Julie responded to its urgency as she must have done before and Penny was left staring at a closed door. She felt rather than heard the shared laughter behind it. This made her position intolerable. She had boasted to Chris that she could go on working with Gerald. Chris had known how impossible it would be. Gerald had no more integrity in the business sense than he had in his personal life. Now she knew that she wasn't an equal partner. As hard as she worked to build up respect, Gerald would smash it down. He needed her, yes. But he needed to destroy her in order to feel king in his world. This was why Laura watched her. Laura knew of Gerald's need to pull Penny down into the mire with him, to make her grovel. When she begged for the crumbs beneath their marriage table, Gerald would be free. This Laura had always known, but had married him in spite of it. This Penny had learned before she left.

She did not leave immediately. That would have been too dramatic. There was no urgency, only a deep thirst for the clean, clear lines of her native countryside. She needed a refuge, but she also needed something more. She needed a place of her own, a place to rest in, to grow in and to be made whole again. All that she needed was waiting for her at Alderbridge and, at the beginning of February, Penny went home. Her parents welcomed her without question, pleased to see her and pleased to fuss over her. Penny was filled with a tender, grateful amusement at their attitude. It was as it had always been. They loved her and were proud of her whatever she had done. Penny Precious! She really was that to her parents and always would be, come what may. Their love made her precious; she had no right to destroy what they cherished. She must find again what it was they held dear and nurture it. It was time now for growing. Deep in the woods, a mile or so outside the village, she found snowdrops, fragile and white yet tough enough to withstand the bitter winds of February. Penny picked a few and sheltered them under the cape sleeves of her bright red coat as she sloshed back through the muddy lanes in her shiny black Wellingtons. How her London friends would laugh to see the latest fashion in topcoats thus accompanied! She'd bought boots specially to match this coat, tall and tight and wrinkling modishly to the calf. Alderbridge lanes would ruin their soft sensuality after one walk, so she'd borrowed her mother's Wellingtons and enjoyed the mud. Now she took more care of the few delicate flowers hidden in her sleeve than of her clothes. She stopped to watch the cows crossing the lane on their way to milking. In the yard, a boy was already washing them down prior to nudging them through to their stalls. Penny could guess what was going on in the long, low milking-shed. Often, she had crept in to watch, to enjoy the sweet-smelling warmth and to be rewarded for her patience by the farmer. It seemed, on reflection, that he'd always had something special to show her — a new calf, a litter of soft puppies or even the first nest of the season. Time had been when she'd vowed to be a farmer's wife. Chris had laughed at that, said she'd burn the cakes and never get the bread to rise. How often they'd finished up in the farmhouse kitchen, eating as though starved! Penny wondered if there was still bread and scones to spare at that scrubbed table presided over by an apple-dumpling of a woman whom the farmer called Peggy. Mrs. Roberts — Penny had met her in the village only this week — had seemed an ideal wife to the sensitive child who had watched her at work. She was always clean, smiling and busy about the house or yard yet, in the village, she was looked up to as the farmer's wife and was always the centre of local activities. She made tea at the long Sunday afternoon cricket matches, always had a cake stall at any Bring and Buy and sang sweet old-fashioned songs at village concerts. On Thursdays she had always visited Grandma's cottage, weighed down with offerings of vegetables, honey and home-made jam. She took no money for these; they were gifts to an old friend unable to do so much for herself as once she'd done. Often she'd spend the afternoon picking blackberries or gooseberries to take away and preserve, but sometimes she sat in the garden with the old lady and told her all the news. This was what Grandma liked best, Penny knew. Once her husband had worked for Mr. Roberts, and his father before him, so she loved to hear about the farm and all the fields. Which field grew barley, which lay summer fallow and what happened to that stretch of land beyond the down, was important to her. Her husband had given his life to these fields and she was content to be part of the land he'd loved. Her life had been narrow but she'd had her man, her children and her cottage and now she had the friendship of her neighbours and the love of her grandchildren. All was well in her little world when Mrs. Roberts chirped on in happy fashion and Penny played in the orchard with Chris.

Remembering all this, Penny arrived at the entrance to her grandmother's cottage as if moved by some force other than her own will. There were no leaves on the tree tunnel leading to the gate, but the holly shrubs and twisted ivy formed a thick hedge that badly needed trimming. There was no fruit or bright sunshine to lure her to the orchard but that was where she went. She found the old swing her father had tied to a strong boughed apple-tree. The rope was wet and soggy but it looked strong enough. Regardless of her coat, she sat on the rough wooden seat. Her feet touched the ground; she'd been much shorter when she'd swung here. Now, she was still, gazing at the immediate earth beneath her feet and remembering. A robin hopped up to her, so close that she could have touched it, and regarded her with its bright eyes. She had nothing to give it, no crumbs at all. There wasn't even a cigarette for herself in her pocket. She and the bird seemed to be a pair, at home here yet watchful, loving the scene before them yet ready to fly. Indeed, a tapping on the cottage window behind them did send the robin darting away and startled Penny out of her reverie. She'd forgotten that the cottage would belong to someone else now. She shouldn't be here. She took one more look around the old orchard then sprang to her feet. She'd have to go and apologise.

Even as she walked towards the cottage, the door opened and a tall figure stooped to come out of it. It was dark in the cottage behind him so Penny did not recognise him at first. Then, he stepped out into the grey February light and Penny could see that it was Chris. Now she wished that, like the robin, she could fly. She, too, would seek the seclusion of the low branches at the other end of the orchard, but she had to stand her ground.

"My! Twopence coloured!" he laughed as he strode towards her.

Penny blushed at his reference to her bright attire. Her hair, too, was swept away under a turban of fur fabric and she could have no idea how like her friend the robin she looked, as bright and gay and yet as wary too.

"I suppose you know you're trespassing, Penny?"

"Yes, I must be. I'd forgotten. I shouldn't have come." Her voice came in short breathless jerks and she couldn't bring herself to face Chris fully. When he spoke again, it was gently as if to soothe her.

"Come back to the swing. I've brought out some scraps for your robin. Let's see if he comes back."

"You saw him?"

"Yes, I was watching you from the window."

"He was so tame. Somebody must feed him. Is anyone living here yet?"

"Not yet."

"Then no one will know we're trespassing?"

"Not unless I tell. Come on — jump up, Penny! I'll give you a push."

"My feet touch the ground now."

"My! How big you've grown! Pick them up, silly."

So Penny picked up her feet and was sent spinning up into the air. The biting wind whipped against her face and made the tears spring to her eyes. She longed to force time back and to be again the girl Chris had pushed on this swing years ago, before she went to London. Then she'd been happy in a life she'd loved, in which there was never any change. Then it had seemed as though there never could be any change. Real tears were blown across her face together with those fashioned by the wind and, when Chris stopped the swing, he mopped her face with his handkerchief.

"You're home now, Penny," he said quietly. "There's no need to go away again, you know."

"I've been such a fool, Chris. I wish I'd never gone away in the first place."

"You had to grow up, Penny. You're quite the lady now."

"Fine raiment isn't all."

"I wasn't thinking about your clothes,

though they're an improvement on the jeans you used to wear."

"Oh, I've learned how to dress and how to behave."

"So bitter, sweet Penny?"

Penny thought long and hard. Was she really bitter or just sad and, if sad, why? Certainly, not because she'd put Gerald behind her. She was sad because her pleasure in being with Chris again was such pain. He was arrogant and masterful and had all the high-handed ways he'd ever had, but her longing to be for him the Penny Precious she could have been was unbearable. She couldn't tell him how she felt, but he must have sensed some anguish in her reply:

"I can't stay here like this, any longer."

"Here?"

"Here, in Alderbridge — hiding away. I can't go on like this. I must do something, any thing."

"Then marry me, Penny."

7

AFTERWARDS Penny never could remember how she replied to that proposal or even how she vacated the swing and hurried home. Against the soft lining of her sleeve, she found one snowdrop head and, brushing it away, wondered where she'd lost the rest. She had fled from Chris like some small child and she waited, expecting him to come chasing after her. All evening her ears were strained to catch the sound of his footsteps and she changed into a soft wool dress for dinner instead of wearing the jeans she usually favoured at home. He didn't come and she went to bed early, not noticing the glances that passed between her parents. They knew better than to question her change of mood, but they recognised a lifting of the weight that had bowed Penny down since her return.

For her part, Penny was bewildered. Why had Chris asked her to marry him? His opinion of her had not been very high lately and she'd done nothing to improve it. Surely Joanna was more his type? She'd seemed possessive enough when Chris had brought her to Avon House. What could have gone wrong? If she'd refused him, then Chris might be looking for an affair on the rebound. But, he'd said 'Marry me'. 'Marry me, Penny', he'd said. Come to think of it, he hadn't asked. As usual, he'd told her what to do. That dictatorial way of his would be his downfall. He'd seen her crying, a waif from a lost love he'd thought and so he'd supplied the answer. Masterfully, he'd solved her problems without caring how she felt. Well, she'd shown him, hadn't she? She'd turned her back on his proposal. She could manage without him. She didn't need his pity.

Next day she busied herself about the little cottage as though her mother had neglected it, polishing and dusting until every corner sparkled. Then, enveloped in one of her mother's huge floral overalls, she attacked the baking. She was lifting the last batch of scones out of the oven when she saw Chris standing in the doorway. To cover her confusion she started to transfer the too-hot scones to a wire tray. Her burnt fingers rebelled and dropped a scone on to the kitchen floor. She bent quickly to retrieve it and sent the whole tray flying with her elbow. She could have screamed with vexation especially as she read the teasing laughter in Chris's eyes.

"Butter fingers this morning!" he quipped as he knelt beside her to help clear up the mess.

"Mind your trousers! There's no need!" Penny protested, then to cover her distress asked:

"What are you doing here, anyway?"

"In the kitchen? You may well ask! I didn't bargain for this, I can tell you."

"Well, then?"

"Well, Penny Plain," and he brushed some flour from her nose as though it annoyed him, "Your father sent me to find you."

"Dad? But he's working."

"He was, but now he's helping your mother polish the sherry glasses."

"What!"

"We're going to celebrate of course. That's why I was tactfully dispatched to find you."

"Tactfully dispatched! What are you talking about?"

"I imagine your parents wanted to give us time for some fond embrace."

"Fond embrace?"

"Can't you do anything more than mimic every word I say? Come here and be kissed, since your parents expect it."

"Certainly not! And why do they expect it? What have you been telling them?"

"I came to ask for your hand in marriage, young lady. It may not seem necessary to a modern miss like you but your father was pleased to discuss my prospects."

"Your what?"

"He is pleased I can keep you in the style to which you have been accustomed, of course."

"You — keep me?"

"Husbands usually do. Stop being so prickly, Penny, and take off that dust-sheet you're wearing. You can't drink to our engagement in that."

Even as she protested, he unfolded the overall from about her and, firmly taking her hand, led her into the sitting-room where her parents were waiting all smiles.

"Penny, you didn't tell us!" her mother chided gently as she kissed her. Before she could reply, Penny felt Chris's arm go round her waist and his fingers bit in warningly as he said, "She was too shy, Mrs. Janes. She begged me to come round last night, but I couldn't make it."

"So that's why she changed her

dress," Mrs. Janes remarked, well satisfied.

"Did you, Penny?" he laughed down into her eyes and his arm tightened momentarily. "You discarded those jeans for me? Would you do it again?"

He laughed outright at her expression.

"Prudish Penny! I only meant would you change to go out."

"Where?"

"Well, we have to buy the ring so I thought a day in Albury might appeal to you."

"Haven't you any work to do?"

"A chap doesn't get engaged every day. I took the day off. We'll go and choose a ring and afterwards I'll take you to lunch. Then I thought it would be nice to book up to take your mother and father somewhere tonight."

"How lovely!" It was her mother who replied. "We ought to have a family party really."

"We will, Mrs. Janes, later. We'll talk it over this evening. But, for today, let's celebrate quietly, shall we?"

Penny's father was watching the scene with quiet amusement and remarked as he handed round the glasses, "That's right, lad! Don't let these women organise you. They've had their own way too long with me."

"Oh, I can cope, sir."

"I see you can. Penny's quieter than I've ever known her."

Penny, seeing her father's dear face alight with happiness, ran to him and threw her arms about him. He held her close for a second before handing her back to Chris.

"Take good care of her, son. She's very precious."

"Penny Precious!" Chris joked as he ruffled her hair. Penny could bear the close intimacy of the atmosphere no longer.

"I must go and change," she declared, knowing that she could never talk this over seriously with Chris until she could get him on his own.

"Something smart! No trousers!" He

admonished as she left the room and she heard her father laughing his approval at this high-handed manner. Alone, she debated whether to wear a trouser suit just to annoy him but settled for something more feminine instead — a dress and coat startlingly simple in dark brown cord. She swept her hair into its severest lines so that for colour and interest her face had no rivals. That her care was appreciated was obvious from the admiring glance that met her when she faced Chris again.

"Well! No robins today, I see!" he bantered lightly but his grip on her arm was firm and, as he put her into the car then lowered his long muscled body into the driving-seat, he whispered, "Fine feathers indeed! Where's my Penny Plain?"

She managed to wave as cheerily as he to her parents, who'd come down to the gate, but as he drew away she countered, "You said something smart."

"I did and you are. You're more than smart, my Penny, you're very lovely."

"Thank you kindly!"

"Don't mock. I thought I'd never seen you so lovely when I saw you at Avon House but, today, I know you have even more to offer."

"You mean you noticed me that night at Avon House?"

"Yes, of course. Who wouldn't?"

"But you had Joanna with you."

"So?"

"Joanna is beautiful, so well groomed, so sophisticated."

"Penny! I do believe you're jealous!"

"Envious perhaps. I certainly can't believe you'd notice me with Joanna around."

"You underestimate yourself, Penny. Don't forget you've always been a part of my life."

"Like an old glove! Comfortable, a good fit, but not exciting."

"What a way to see yourself. I can tell we shall have to change all this."

"But I don't want to be like Joanna!"

He drove in silence for a while, but, when they came to a sheltered cul-de-sac on the country lane, he pulled in and stopped. His voice was rough and masterful when he said, "Let's get this straight. I'm marrying you, not anyone else."

"But why? Why not Joanna?"

"I don't want to hear about Joanna, ever again. Do you understand?"

He was holding her by the shoulders and shaking her as he spoke.

"But — "

"But nothing! No more about Joanna. Be yourself!"

"I'm sorry, Chris. I won't mention her again."

"That's better! Now any more doubts? Let's hear them all now."

So Joanna had hurt him. He couldn't bear to mention her. Perhaps this marriage was as much to help him save face as her. Dare she ask?

"Chris, please don't be cross, but why?"

"Why what?"

"Why have you asked me to marry you? You don't have to you know. The worst is over for me."

"That, my dear, is why. Because it's over. I couldn't have married you while you were hankering after that Gerald, but now I need you."

"You need me?"

"Yes, Penny. You've never asked about my job. Do you know what it is?"

"Gerald said you were our youngest tycoon."

"Did he now?"

"Yes — a dynamo, he said. So you must do something in the business world."

"I do. So far I've been successful. Young, yes. Forceful. Dynamic, if you like. Now I need to change my image, capture the mature eye, too. I need to settle down."

"Settle down!"

"Don't laugh, Penny, or I'll beat you! I mean that I mustn't be seen to be playing the field any more. I need to be married."

"And not to Joanna?"

"God damn it, woman! I told you before! Not Joanna, now or ever."

"I see."

"Do you, Penny? Do you really see? Do you know why you have to marry me? I can't afford to give you time to change your mind. I need a wife now."

"For business reasons?"

"For that and for myself. The time has come to make changes. There is a time for everything. It is time for me to marry and I want you to be my wife."

"Not because you're sorry for me?"

"Your friend Gerald could have told you that tycoons — however young — never succeed by acting out of pity."

"Then?"

"It's you I want, Penny. A girl who can relax in jeans at home yet look like an angel on formal occasions. You don't need sophistication. You've got a natural dignity that will carry you head high into my life."

"You need a hostess?"

"I need you! Will you marry me, Penny? Say yes now, without being hustled, now that you know the score."

He had obviously built an empire with the idea of Joanna beside him. Now he needed that partner and Joanna had let him down. Poor Chris. Well, she knew what it was like to be used. At least, she could help Chris. She had something to give him.

"Yes, Chris. I'll marry you."

"With no regrets?"

"Regrets?"

"I was going to say regrets about Gerald. But let's put Gerald behind us with Joanna. I'll settle for what you have to give."

"And I."

"You! You needn't worry. I'll always have prospects. You'll have nothing to worry about."

She wanted to remind him of that

part of himself he'd given to Joanna. She'd be settling for less of him than he cared to acknowledge. However, she'd promised not to mention Joanna again.

"Let's both forget yesterday. This is a new day and we're getting engaged."

"Kiss me then and seal the bargain."

But they didn't kiss because she buried her head in his chest and he held her tightly and spoke over her head.

"Don't let this thing with Gerald make you undervalue yourself, Penny. Stand tall again!"

"You should talk! You've always teased me about being so small."

"Stop that! Nobody calls my wife small."

"But I'm not your wife yet."

"We'd better remedy that or I won't answer for the consequences."

"Let's get engaged first then."

"A mere formality!" He whispered into her hair, but it was he who put her from him and straightened his tie.

"There's a mirror on the back of

your sun visor," he instructed, his tone making it sound like an admonishment to tidy her hair. She must have flushed in her vexation, for he grinned and explained, "Can't stand women who use my driving mirror."

"I wasn't going to," she countered and flipped open her handbag to reveal a small mirror on the inside flap. With its aid she restored her former grooming, trying to ignore Chris's watchful amusement.

"Honour satisfied?" he asked lightly when she closed the bag.

"Quite," she returned, determined to match his bantering mood.

Formality or not, the ring was chosen with care. Penny was delighted with the diamond that finally sparkled from her third finger, but she was left with the feeling that her choice had been manoeuvred. A little blue cluster the shape of a forget-me-not and the colour of hyacinths had appealed to her, but Chris dismissed it with a shrug. After that she deliberately let her choice come from the most expensive selection and knew from Chris's grin that that had been his original intention. So with the rest of the day, lunch, dinner and dancing to follow. Recklessly she tried to outbid the banker but he seemed delighted to let her win. Her mother attempted to curb her extravagance over dinner but Chris would have none of it. There was more than a glint of devilment in those tawny eyes as he let her see that the master could afford to call the tune.

As there had been no question about a formal engagement so there was none about where the wedding would take place. Bride and groom had been born in Alderbridge and christened at the parish church. There they would be married at Easter. Penny did not favour the idea of a big white wedding, but Chris was firm.

"Your mother will expect it so that's what she'll get."

"But it's my wedding, not my mother's!"

"It's mine too, my girl, and it can't be a quiet affair. The press will be there."

"And Christopher Lloyd's bride mustn't be suspected of hiding a broken heart! She must be virginal in white!"

There was a sneer in Penny's voice but Chris was quietly adamant, refusing to be drawn. "Let's have it before the altar with all the trappings," he insisted, his magnetic eyes searching her soul. Why was he mocking her? Did he think that her love-making with Gerald had gone further than it had? How dared he compare her with Joanna! His face, though, was inscrutable as he insisted, "Most brides are beautiful, but mine will be the loveliest the most radiant in the whole world."

"Why? Nobody has any doubts about your love affairs, do they? It's all very well for the man!"

"Yes, but my wife will be seen to be above suspicion."

"Chauvinist pig!"

He dismissed the matter with a laugh, not bothering to deny the implication. After that Penny never mentioned the wedding dress but she went to endless trouble to find the frostiest white she could. Her dressmaker demurred at the unrelieved tone and begged to be allowed to soften the crisp lace with a cream underlayer. Penny did not weaken. She would go to Chris looking like an untouched snowflake, crystal white. Whatever his suspicion she still warranted a white wedding. Even the orchids she chose to carry were white, veined only with the creamiest green.

If Penny had harboured the idea that her betrothal would be a period of pleasant courtship, she was mistaken. The morning after their engagement, Chris rang to ask her if she could meet him for lunch.

"Again? Really, Chris! Are you going to make a habit of it?"

"On the contrary, my Penny. I have to leave for New York tomorrow."

"Oh!"

She felt let down as if all the events of yesterday had been some elaborate charade. Chris's voice was amused as he added, "Don't worry! I'll be back for the wedding."

"How kind!"

"Stop that! Or I may change my mind and marry you by special licence before I go."

"Think of the press!"

"I was thinking of myself. Now, for your sauce, you can languish in Alderbridge while I live it up in America."

"Well, I certainly shan't have time to languish. I've too much to settle before Easter."

"Yes, that's really why I want to see you at lunchtime. I've made an appointment for us to see Mr. Limpeney this afternoon."

"But I told you before! Mr. Limpeney isn't my solicitor any more. I can handle the outstanding business with Gerald myself, thank you."

"My little spitfire! I've no desire to come between you and Gerald in your business deals, but I do want you to come and see Mr. Limpeney with me."

"Why — "

"Wait and see!"

He would say no more so Penny had to agree to meet him for lunch.

She was amazed that, instead of driving into town, he took the road to her grandmother's cottage. He was as tense as a coiled spring as he led her down the path and put his hand in his pocket for the key. Penny didn't say a word as he turned the key in the lock and stood back to let her go in before him.

"Oh, Chris!" she exclaimed at last when she had fully taken in the clean and shining room into which he had guided her. Someone had cared for this room lovingly and a log-fire caught the gleam of polished furniture and picked out the rich greens and reds of the chintz. Penny knelt before the huge open fireplace and asked: "Who lit the fire?"

"I did."

"You?"

She sounded so incredulous that he jumped to his own defence: "Well, I lit it often enough for your grandmother."

"Yes, but — "

"But what?"

"Now you have servants to do things for you."

"I did this for you."

"This?"

"Yes, tried to make this room look as you remembered it — as we remember it."

"Oh, Chris! How lovely!"

Jumping up, she planted a kiss at the corner of his mouth and, matching her mood, he swung her up in a brotherly bear-hug.

"Be warned, though!"

"Of what?"

"I only managed this room. The rest of the house is rather neglected."

"But whose is it now, Chris?"

He looked at her strangely, as if he would delve the very depths of her soul for a reaction as he replied, "Yours, Penny."

"Mine!"

"Yes, Penny. That's why I want you to see Mr. Limpeney. I shouldn't have told you yet, but this New York business has altered all my plans."

"How can it be mine, Chris?" she asked like a small child who'd been offered the contents of a toyshop and found herself overwhelmed to the point of disbelief.

"It's my wedding present to you, Penny."

"Then you own it now?"

"I bought it, yes, but only our marriage lies between you and the ownership."

"A bribe?"

"Penny! How could you? Did I offer it to you before you took my ring?"

"No, Chris. I'm sorry. I shouldn't have said that. But I still can't understand."

"Sit down, Penny, and I'll explain."

Instinctively, Penny curled up in her familiar position on the hearthrug, her head resting against an armchair. Chris took the rocking-chair that had been Grandma's favourite and so kept a distance between them.

"Penny, do you remember that I came to view this cottage on the day of the sale?"

"With Joanna, yes."

"We came to consider its possibilities as a small guesthouse or hotel."

"But why?"

"It was your field of business and I wanted to be able to impress on you that you had an asset here."

"You mean that you bothered about me even then?"

"I always bothered about you, child. You plagued the life out of me. Remember?"

"Yes — but then I was going to marry Gerald."

"Oh, I never believed in that!" he declared airily. "Anyway, the cottage was a good investment whatever happened. Joanna saw its possibilities at once."

Of course, the renovations! She'd heard him mention them to Joanna on the day of the sale. So they had planned to buy the cottage for themselves. He wouldn't admit it now, of course. Would they have lived here?

As if guessing the drift of her thoughts, Chris continued: "After we're married, we'll live at Grange House, of course." Of course! He wouldn't want to live in the little love-nest he and Joanna had chosen would he.

"Are you listening, Penny?"

"Yes of course."

"Then do cheer up. You look as though we're discussing your funeral not your wedding plans."

"Wedding?"

"Yes, Penny, wedding plans! After we're married I want you still to have an interest of your own."

"Oh!"

"Does that surprise you? Did you

think I'd monopolise you body and soul?"

"Not exactly, but — "

"Chauvinist pig, wasn't it? Your imagination must have been working overtime about our married life!"

She flushed beneath his bantering gaze and he grinned broadly.

"So! Well, I'm sorry to disappoint you, my little slave girl, but there'll be times when I won't be around. You'll need something else to fill that little head."

"A job you mean?"

"Not exactly. An interest, I'd prefer to call it. I'm often called away at a moment's notice and, like now, I'm heavily committed for weeks on end. Somehow I don't see you as the dutiful little wife waiting for my return. I'd like to think you had this place to keep you out of mischief."

"Can't I come with you?"

"On business trips? No."

"Why not?"

"I need all my wits about me, Penny.

I can't afford to be worrying about what scrapes you're getting into in faraway places."

"I could go sightseeing."

"I'll take you sightseeing when you go. I don't want you wandering around foreign parts on your own."

"Oh!"

"Again that oh! Come now, Penny, I'm giving you a chance to prove your talents."

"How?"

"Take this place, Grandma's old cottage, and turn it into a success."

"Like Avon House?"

"If you like."

"No. I don't like! I know just what this place needs and what kind of people would come here."

"Good! Can you work quickly? You have a couple of hours to go over the place and roughly estimate the cost of alterations."

"Why?"

"I want to make you a gift of the cottage together with enough money to set the venture going. We need to do some sums before we meet Mr. Limpeney."

"But I have the money from Avon House. I'd rather use that."

"Never! Spend it on your trousseau."

"Don't be ridiculous!"

"I want you to have lovely clothes, Penny. You'll need your money."

"Keeping up appearances again?"

"If you like, but there's to be no penny-pinching about it."

"Penny-pinching!" Her sense of the ridiculous sent her into gales of laughter and, joining her amusement, Chris jumped to his feet and stretched down a hand to pull her up too.

"Come! Let's look round before lunch."

Together, they toured the cottage they both remembered so well and Penny's enthusiasm for its conversion was catching.

"Can we build on to it, Chris?"

"I don't see why not. Why, what do you want? It's a big place as it is."

"Yes, plenty of bedrooms, but I'd like a huge sun lounge looking out over the garden."

"Good idea! And you could have modern kitchens built in on that side while you're at it."

"Then we need a room big enough for receptions, even dancing."

"Why?"

"It would catch on with the villagers. The church hall is rather bare and do-it-yourself. This could become the in-place for wedding receptions, parties and celebrations."

"You have a free hand, Penny. It's yours and so is the money you eventually make from it."

From then on Penny was too engrossed in plans, sketches and estimates even to notice a van draw up at the gate and Chris's departure to meet it. She was Penny, involved in her work again, until Chris called:

"Lunch is served. Come and get it!"

She'd expected to be whisked away

to a restaurant and was so pleased to see the cups of hot soup and the boxes of chicken and chips. With papers spread out around them they went on planning alterations and costing them as they ate. Penny was amazed to discover how well she worked with Chris, how their ideas matched and complemented each other. In this field, his domineering manner was gone and she felt a partnership that she'd never known with him before. Absently, her hand moved among the paper in her picnic-box and, in dismay, she saw that she had eaten every scrap. And she was still hungry! Watching her, Chris laughed:

"Penny! How do you stay so slim?"

"Mmmmmm?"

"Never mind. Keep at it. I've got something else in the car." He was back in minutes with a flask and a white paper-bag.

"Come on, Penny! Break for coffee."

He'd even remembered to bring coffee and in the bag were two delicious looking cream doughnuts.

"Ooh scrumptious!"

"I remembered you liked them."

Penny liked this new relaxed mood they had discovered together and was sorry when the time came to leave the cottage and drive to the solicitor's office. Once there, Chris was business-like and efficient so that, by the end of the afternoon, the matter of her wedding present was settled. In the car, Chris said, "I'm sorry, Penny, but I'll have to take you home now. There's so much to settle this evening."

"Oh, Chris! And I haven't even thanked you properly!"

"Well?" Penny caught a glimpse of his smile and, without warning, her heart lurched. She tried to remove her glance from his but it was ensnared by something in his eyes, something deeper than the amusement. With a worn grin, he said:

"Come here, you dear, sweet, adorable little fool."

As he drew her into his arms, Penny

melted against him. His lips found hers. They lingered long and tenderly. When he put her from him, he said softly, "When I get back, it'll be only three days until our honeymoon."

"Must you be so long, Chris?"

"Under the circumstances, I think it's just as well, young lady!"

A weakness at what she saw in his eyes engulfed her and cut off her speech. His breath was still warm on her face and his hands exploring her shoulders, his fingers sinking into her flesh, then he was jerking up straight and saying gruffly, "We'll pick up this thread again. Preferably when the honeymoon's closer! Right now, I think we'd better get away from these windows!"

Penny looked out to see a thick thatch of white hair disappear swiftly from over the half lace curtain at the solicitor's window. Feeling the tension within her snap, she shook inwardly then, unable to contain herself any longer, doubled up with laughter. Chris, seeing the funny side of it too, began to grin and drove off noisily, hooting his horn in a farewell gesture to the old man who knew them both better than they realised.

8

PENNY had just rushed in from her last fitting with the dressmaker and grabbed a fresh roll which she was busily stuffing with ham and salad from the fridge when the phone rang. Taking the food with her, she picked up the receiver and was met with such a medley of sounds that she took a large bite of the roll while waiting for the line to clear. She was chewing happily when Chris's voice came through loud and clear.

"Hello, darling!"

Swallowing guiltily at being caught, she choked on a crumb and could hardly splutter out a greeting.

"Penny? What are you doing? No, don't tell me. Eating again!"

Even on a bad line, Penny caught the hint of gentleness in his teasing voice. It brought a lump to her throat and she longed to see him again.

"Chris! When are you coming home?"

"Miss me?"

"Mmmmmm." She was glad he couldn't see the tell-tale flush in her cheeks that revealed so much.

"Good! That's how it should be!"

She wanted to ask him if he missed her but she was too shy to venture such a question. Stupidly, she had nothing to say.

"Lost your tongue, Penny?"

"No."

"Nothing to tell me?"

"Well, everything's ready for Saturday if that's what you want to know."

"That'll do for a start. So now it only remains for me to get home?"

"Yes. There are only three days, Chris. When are you coming?"

"Tomorrow, my pet."

"Oh good!"

She couldn't keep the pleasure out of her voice and she heard him laugh softly at the other end.

"My flight gets in at noon, Penny.

I'll be in Alderbridge at four. Let's meet at the cottage, shall we?"

"Oh, yes! Chris, I've got so much to show you there."

"Already?"

"Yes, it's so exciting. I'm longing for you to see it."

"And I'm longing to see you!"

"Oh, Chris!"

"Tomorrow then? At the cottage."

"Yes."

"Until then, my love."

"Goodbye, Chris."

"See you tomorrow, precious.

Clinging to his words, trying to read into them a declaration of love, Penny waited until the line was quite dead before she returned the receiver to its cradle. Only then did she remember that she was going up to London herself the next day. There were several last-minute items of shopping that had to be done, orders to be picked up and a visit to her solicitor to be made. If only she'd told Chris, she could have met him at the airport. How lovely to see him at lunch-time, instead of a whole afternoon later! Well, there was nothing to stop her. She would go up early in the morning, finish all her shopping then surprise Chris by meeting him off the plane. It would be nice to see his face light up when he saw her. Penny found that she could hardly wait. The night seemed so long and she was up with the dawn, walking down to the cottage to check that it was just as she wanted Chris to see it. To her, it was more like her future home than she could ever imagine Grange House being. Chris and she had never discussed their future there so she had no enthusiasm for it. To the cottage, though, she lent all her energies, caring more for its renovation than for her wedding preparations. This morning she found the tranquillity there to steady her so that, by breakfast-time, she was outwardly calm. Her mother did not remark on her early-morning excursion but bullied her into eating a large breakfast before her father drove her down to the station.

Penny saw Chris before he had a chance to see her. How grateful she was for that, afterwards. Her first glimpse of him, tall, bronzed and incredibly handsome, sent a thrill of pleasure surging through her. He was coming home to her. Pride bubbled up inside her to mingle with the joy. Then, she saw Joanna! Almost as tall as Chris, her slim form jostled against him as the stream of passengers hurried along. They stood out in the crowd, a striking couple with eyes only for each other. They were talking animatedly and every so often they slowed to a near pause to face each other in conversation. Penny could almost hear that deep chocolate voice as it crooned in Chris's ear. So he'd taken Joanna with him! Penny clung to the shelter her pillar afforded her while she tried to recover from the shock. She had only to step forward to be recognised, to claim her fiancé, but she could not move. She let them pass close to her, so close that she felt the warmth of Joanna's perfume in her nostrils and still they did not see her. She followed them from a distance, feeling like some furtive schoolgirl spying on a pair of lovers, until Chris hailed a taxi. Then Joanna lifted up her face to his and, as he bent to kiss her, her arms crept round his neck in a fond caress. Penny could not see any reluctance on his part to share the embrace. Only three days to his wedding and he was kissing someone else. She didn't wait to see any more but stumbled away to walk the streets and try to understand.

She was still walking at four o'clock, the time she was to have met Chris. He'd be there now at the cottage. He'd wonder where she was. Well, let him! He'd taken Joanna on his trip to New York after telling Penny, herself, that she'd only be a nuisance. So that was why she wouldn't be welcome on trips! He could still make it with Joanna if he left his wife behind. Wife! She wasn't his wife yet. She'd show him. She'd stay in London and let him search for his wife-to-be. Let the press find out! Determined, Penny found herself a hotel and booked in, then she rang her mother.

"I've met some friends," she lied blandly, "so I'm staying overnight."

"But, Penny! Chris has been demented. He's been hunting everywhere for you. Can't you get back tonight?"

"No."

"What shall I tell him?"

"Tell him, I'll see him at the church."

"Penny! At least give me a number he can ring."

Penny chose not to hear that and rang off before her mother could question her closely.

By the next morning, cold reason had taken the place of anger. Penny had spent the whole night struggling with the problem. It would be a fine defiant gesture to leave Chris with a wedding and no bride. He deserved it. But, it would be the very end, no more Chris and no more cottage to build into a hotel. Love had denied her a partner once, taken away all that she had cared about. Could she let it happen again? What was love, anyway? It was that quick response to his touch, that half-drowsy desire, that awareness of a passionate force being held in check. It was that irresistible burn of ice on the skin and the full passion of sunlight that made one feel that this was what life was all about. But that was all for the romantics. She could do without the peachy delights. Why let Chris Lloyd have his cake and eat it as well? She could still show him! There'd be the cottage to convert and plenty for her to do. Ted and June were coming for the wedding. She had planned to persuade them to come down to Alderbridge and help her in the new project. Ted was just the manager she needed. She would make a success of the Cottage Hotel and she'd be the perfect wife for a businessman. Chris need have no reason to complain.

He'd have the wife he deserved and he could satisfy his more passionate nature elsewhere. He'd had no fine scruples before so he could continue to take his pleasure with Joanna.

By lunchtime, a very tired but determined Penny was back in Alderbridge. She didn't go straight home. She felt that she couldn't face her mother's concern just yet. Instead, she went to her grandmother's cottage, letting herself in the back way with the key Mr. Limpeney had given her. Again, she went into that familiar room at the front and her throat was tight and aching. A voice shattered the composure she was struggling so hard to find.

"So! You're here at last!"

Those tones! Her pulses flying, Penny whirled round and gasped, "Chris! Wh-what are you doing here?"

He let his gaze slide slowly over her, taking in the suitcase and the lack of sleep in her eyes. His face became a mask of fury.

"Where have you been?"

Penny's cheeks flamed. So, he was thinking the worst of her! Because she hadn't been here to meet him, he believed she'd been seeing Gerald. He'd never trust her. Well, that was all right because now she didn't trust him. Angry and hurt to the point of tears, she faced him and snapped:

"That's none of your business!"

His jaw flexed thunderously, his arm was raised as if to hit her but, even as she flinched away, his hand whipped out to take her wrist and jerk her to him. Penny panicked at his nearness. She struggled wildly to escape as he demanded:

"Well, did you see him? Is that why you weren't here as we arranged?"

"No. Let go of me!"

His tightened grip shot through her like a searing pain. She shook her arm and snapped crossly, "Why shouldn't I see him? You weren't here."

His gaze smouldered menacingly as he watched her work herself into a frenzy of rage.

"So! When I'm away, you're going to look up the old flame, eh?"

"You had Joanna!"

"What?"

The one word rapped out like a pistol shot. Penny hadn't meant to mention Joanna but her fury had robbed her of caution. She struggled wildly to escape, telling him shakily:

"I saw you. I saw you with Joanna. At the airport. You can't deny it."

"I don't deny it," he drawled with a peculiar smile. "I was with Joanna. Is that why you stayed in London?"

"Why shouldn't I? Why shouldn't I go to Gerald?"

His strength was overpowering as he pulled her closer to him.

"Did you, Penny? Did you go to Gerald?"

"It isn't your business! I saw you kissing Joanna. Why should you bother who I went to?"

She felt the anger in him as he sneered, "So this is what you wanted?"

Pinned in his embrace, she could

do nothing as he brought his mouth down roughly on to hers. Nor did she want to. This kindled a desire in her that Gerald had never made her feel. This was what she had been waiting all her life for. Exultantly, she let her lips reply. She didn't want him to stop as his mouth savagely explored hers. It was only when a sweet trembling filled her limbs that sanity returned. Fool! Fool! She shouted at her heart. Hadn't she with her own eyes seen Chris kissing someone else? Though his kiss meant everything to her, for him she was but a substitute for Joanna. And she had let him think she'd spent the night with Gerald! Convinced now that his lips held nothing but contempt for her, she broke free of him. For a moment she stood facing him with angry tears in her eyes. His haggard expression came as something of a shock to her. She could clearly see the effect of her disappearance on him. He hadn't slept either. There was something else there too, as he watched her, something like pain. But she only wanted to hurt him so she ignored the appeal in his eyes and said, "I shall sue!"

His face darkened then he asked quite calmly, "Sue for what?"

She should have been warned by his quiet tones, but she blundered on: "For breach of promise, of course. Don't think you're going to get out of it easily."

"There'll be no breach of promise, Penny," he stated in a deadly calm that took the breeze out of her sails completely as she spoiled for a fight.

"But for God's sake keep out of my way until after the wedding or I'll be tempted to break every bone in your body!"

Unable to resist goading him farther, Penny asked, "And after the wedding?"

"You'd better learn to look after yourself!"

He turned and strode out of the room. The outside door slammed. The room was empty.

"Chris!" Through a blaze of tears, she ran out to the long path down to the gate, but it was too late. Chris was getting into his car and it slid away. Choking back a sob, Penny stumbled inside and collapsed into the rocking-chair. Why hadn't she defended herself? Why had she let Chris think that she'd been with Gerald? After all, Chris had been in the wrong and she'd let him put all the blame on her. Why did she always let her silly pride prevent her from telling the truth? Jealousy of Joanna had kept her in London. It had nothing to do with Gerald. She lay back in the chair for a while then rose and tidied herself up. She had to go home. She was getting married on Saturday and there was so much to do. Nothing had changed.

Penny's wedding-day dawned bright but cold. Having forced herself to smile her way through the last few days, Penny woke feeling that she could never smile again. Her mother was distressed at her pallor and fussed over her, insisting that she have breakfast in bed and try to get some rest. For the first time since Chris proposed, there was nothing to do. Everything was ready. It only remained to get herself dressed for the ceremony and to teach her face to smile. Her wedding gown was hanging in the wardrobe in all its icy glory and her packed suitcases were standing in one corner of the room. There was no bridesmaid to come to help her dress so Penny started early, whiling away half an hour in a long, deep bath. Any other time, she would have luxuriated in the soft warm fragrance of the water but today was different. She wanted to force the morning forwards, to get to the service and to have it over. She hadn't spoken to Chris alone since they'd met at the cottage. Always, he'd come when there were people about, kissing her briefly in greeting so that no one could doubt their love. She had taken it all coolly, even lovelier in her self-imposed calm, but dismissing any gesture of intimacy.

Sometimes her outward composure had startled him, making him suddenly no more than an awkward boy, he who had always been so suave and confident. She knew that this angered him and, while she enjoyed the power it gave her as a woman, she feared his reaction when they must at last be alone. It would have been better if she had not acknowledged her awareness of him as a man. As it was, she had concentrated on looking and behaving like a nun while deliberately flaunting the knowledge of her womanhood. In his eyes she had seen the warning lights that spoke of his revenge. Yet the final power would be hers. The thought of it kept her calm, causing her to draw into herself. Often her mouth would tighten into a secret smile. She had a weapon in herself. He would not be proof against it. Already she had seen her magic call the colour into his face, set a stammer into his speech. She knew he was not a cold or patient man. He would want her; she had seen the desire leap in his eyes at her new demure grace, but she would never be his. Probably, even at this moment as she bathed and he got ready at Grange House, he was thinking of the promise in her innocent eyes. Well, it was a promise she had put there deliberately, an innocence she had assumed. She had no intention of sharing his bed tonight or any other night. She couldn't wait for the opportunity to tell him so.

Penny's only moment of weakness came after her mother had left for the church. Alone in the cottage she had grown up in, with the father who had watched her grow, she knew that she shouldn't be marrying Chris in this spirit. Her father's eyes seemed moist with unshed tears as he realised her loveliness. He took both her hands in his and carried them to his lips. She faltered and would have fallen into his arms but he held her hands firmly, telling her gently:

"You must not spoil your dress now.

Be still, my little Penny Precious. You are doing the right thing."

"But, Dad!" In her agitation, she would have told him all, how Chris didn't love her and she was only second best, stand in for another woman. But, she could not fill him with her doubts. His pain was at losing a child. She could not make it greater by revealing the kind of future he had lost her to. He was so sure for her when he said, "Listen, the car is coming. It's time to go."

She went with him to the door but could not step out into the morning. Inside this cottage, all love and warmth were united. Outside, the day was cold.

"Come," her father said gently, "Chris is waiting."

He put his hand under the white blaze of lace that shimmered out from her elbow and led her to the car. Streets and people were a haze to her as they drove the short distance to the church. It seemed as though everyone in the village had turned out to see her wed and she had to return their wishes with smiles. Tears brightened her eyes, but, once at the church, those droplets froze into icy stillness. There, in the crowd round the porch, was Joanna! Her gaze at Penny was an interested summing look and her smile was somewhere between triumph and contempt. She had not been invited by Penny's parents. Penny herself had helped prepare every invitation. What did Chris mean then by asking her personally? Had he so little feeling for his bride?

Penny must have tripped, for she felt her father's hand steadying her and was content to lean on him as the photographers began their work. She didn't pause long for them, just long enough to regain her composure. When she came into the darkness of the little church, she had no idea what the long plain gown did for her. It sent every eye to her face where her skin was pale as marble. Her large eyes glowed so blue as to be almost black and her hair shone rosy fair. It swept sleekly up into a crystal coronet that held no more colour than the blush of mother-of-pearl. She saw the shock of admiration on Chris's face as he turned and took in her beauty, then she saw his eyes darken with anger. She had no way of knowing that this masked his concern at her pallor. She was still as their eyes locked momentarily before the service began. The scent in the church of Easter flowers, catkins, primroses and violets was sweet in a way that was to twist in her memory ever afterwards. Regret mingled with love as she spoke her vows and they were made man and wife. There was no turning back. They were signing their names in the vestry, laughing into a kiss for the photographers and running beneath a hail of confetti to reach the shelter of the car. The drive to the village hall was brief and Penny realised she'd hardly stopped smiling before the whole act started again at the reception. Chris was greeting everyone gaily. Well, if he could act, so could she! She would let everybody see how much she loved this handsome new husband of hers. There would be no room for doubt. She took his hand and smiled up into his eyes. He gave a brief flash of anger before he, too, decided to play the game. Or was he blinded to her deceit? Now, eye answered eye, his silence became the answer to her flirting and each long look burned between them. His was an excitement longing to be quenched in her body that night. She knew it and fanned the flame. The greater his need then the harder the fall when she denied him his pleasure. Penny was swept up in a secret exultation as fierce as anger only more triumphant. As she threw herself into her part, a dimple deepened prettily then disappeared on her cheek and her eyelashes drooped sweetly then fanned upwards into a wide gaze. Her colour now was high, pretty in comparison with the ethereal pallor of earlier on. To the guests she had now become approachable, a graceful bride tilting a smiling face to her new husband. No one doubted that he was anything but completely captivated by her feminine magic.

Chris drove her back to the cottage to change, since there were no facilities at the hall.

"See how much more convenient we could make it at the Cottage Hotel," Penny explained nervously, talking fast to cover her confusion at being alone with him.

"What's wrong with this?" murmured Chris, absently brushing a whisp of fair hair back up into her coronet, then weaving his arms around her waist and gazing down at her.

"Here we are together and all the guests at least a mile away. It's perfect."

He could spoil all her good intentions now, Penny realised. She broke away from his embrace, hurrying upstairs, excusing herself as she went.

"But the time, Chris! We'll never get away!"

"Does it matter?"

"Of course. We're travelling by train, aren't we?"

"Only to London."

He was standing inside her tiny bedroom watching her as she unfastened the coronet and shook her hair free of its restraint.

"Chris! What are you doing here? This is my bedroom."

"Yes, and we're married now, aren't we?"

She flushed brightly beneath his scrutiny as she struggled with the zip of her wedding dress.

"Here, let me."

His hand took one shoulder and he slid the zip down, letting the frosty white lace fall from her like a veil. Suddenly shy and unsure how to handle the situation she stepped out of the clouds of prim material and bent to pick it up.

"I'll do that," Chris offered. "You'd

better get changed before I decide that even London is too far."

When she saw that he really intended to hang up her dress, she allowed herself a soft flirtatious laugh before disappearing into the bathroom where she hurriedly changed into underclothes more suitable for her going away suit. When she returned to her bedroom, she was almost demurely clad in a white slip that neatly covered her slim form. Chris looked up from his examination of her dressing table and said:

"Why so shy, Penny mine?"

"I-I'm not shy — exactly."

"Exactly! That's great! Penny, you're like a little bird struggling to escape."

He came to her and gathered her close, his hand cupping her left breast. "Penny! Your heart's drumming! You're not afraid of me, are you?"

"Of course not. It's just that we'll be missed if we take too long."

He nuzzled his head between her breasts then, in one movement, spread her across the covers of her narrow bed. As his mouth tasted her soft flesh, he whispered softly, "There's time enough, Penny," and he cradled her body to him.

"No, Chris! Not here!"

A quick control came down over his ardour. He lifted himself up on one elbow and his face had gone rigid.

"Is it so repugnant to you then, that it shouldn't be here?" He was standing up before she could answer and taking restless strides across the room then back again.

"Would you blame me for ever if I took you here?"

"Blame you?"

"Yes, blame me. The blame is mine. The time is right but not the place. Here you are too much your father's daughter."

He stopped pacing suddenly and stood squarely in front of her. "Get up! That abandoned pose doesn't become you."

"Chris!"

"Get up, I say. Don't lie there

wide-legged and inviting me. That's what you've been doing all afternoon — inviting me. Well, you can stop it now. Get dressed and come downstairs."

He left the room and she heard him storm down the stairs. As quickly as her trembling fingers would allow, she made herself ready to join him. She had chosen grey for her going-away outfit, a soft suit of dove colour trimmed with the red of cherries. Her hair was supposed to be caught up in a swathe of cherry velvet but, when the time came to arrange it, she lacked her usual dexterity. Instead, she let her hair fall loose and shining, catching it back from her brow with the broad band of bright velvet. It was enough. She needed no other adornments. Her only jewellery was the new gold ring on her left hand and, above it, the diamond Chris had chosen.

When she went downstairs, Chris's gaze flicked over her swiftly before he asked:

"Where is your luggage?"

"Upstairs. I'll fetch it."

"No," he snapped. "Leave it. I'll go myself. You'd better go out to the car so that we can leave straight away."

She didn't go immediately but let her eyes wander round the room she had loved so much. It wasn't her home any more; she had to make a new one. She stood by the window collecting her thoughts and missed the long curious look Chris gave her as he carried out her cases. She never glanced his way or guessed what he might see so she was surprised by the understanding in his voice as he said:

"Come now. There's no point in making yourself so sad."

Her voice was low in reply. "I'm ready," was all she said and she walked out to the car, slight but erect with a grace of which she was totally unaware.

This natural grace carried her through the final farewells at the hall and kept her calm and composed throughout the journey to London. Chris chatted in a friendly manner about the hotel suite he'd booked for the night. They were only staying in London for one night then flying off to the sun the next day. Penny wondered whether Chris would want to cancel the rest of the honeymoon when he knew her terms. For now, he seemed to have forgotten the incident in the cottage and was friendly and charming. If he found her withdrawn or aloof, he didn't comment. He seemed to go out of his way to make allowances for her quiet manner and, as soon as they were in their room, he suggested to Penny that she have a tray of tea then a rest on the bed while he made some business calls from downstairs. There was only one small overnight bag to unpack so she took his advice gladly. Stretched out on one of the two single beds, she reflected how easy it would be once she'd rejected him. He wouldn't have to take a blanket and sleep on the floor! Thank heaven for twin beds! She was civilised enough to let him sleep in his as long as he left her alone.

She hadn't expected to fall asleep or to respond so readily to the kiss that woke her. She cradled the head that nuzzled into her shoulder and shuddered with the joy that his blind mouth searching her flesh aroused. The filmy robe she had so deliberately chosen fell open to reveal soft rounded curves and she felt his warm hovering breath. A weakness engulfed her until, realising what it meant, she broke wildly free of him. All too clearly she could see the flames in his eyes darken. There was something else there too as he watched her, something like a spark of pain. She didn't want to see that. He'd hurt her so much that now all she wanted was to hurt him in return. As if to destroy the desire he'd made her feel, she raised her hand to strike him but he caught it before she reached his face and held her pinioned on the bed. His mood had changed without warning. Before, he'd been sprawled over her in an abandonment of pleasure; now he was taut with tension and held her roughly pinned in an embrace that was far from tender.

"Well! What is all this? Why so edgy? Is it just nerves, my Penny?

"No, Chris, it's not. It wasn't nerves at home and it isn't nerves now."

She felt the shock of that coil through him before he released her and sat up. His voice was cold though his eyes still smouldered as he said, "You'd better explain. When you turned cold on me back in your home, I was annoyed. But then, I blamed myself for my unfeeling choice of place."

"Unfeeling! You are unfeeling! Who else would have invited his mistress to his wedding?"

"What?"

His eyes had gone hard and there seemed to be more than anger in him, driving him on. "Penny, I could have killed Gerald with my bare hands, but that doesn't mean I took a mistress in spite. You have nothing to complain of in my behaviour."

"I have. She was there at the church, smiling as if she'd won."

"Who was?"

"Joanna, of course. The same Joanna you took on your trip though you couldn't take me. Your little bit on the side!"

"Don't be so coarse, Penny. It doesn't become you. I was sorry for the way I spoke to you this afternoon in your bedroom. But, by God, you ask for it! Like so many women, my dear wife, you have a touch of the tart in you. You've been leading me on all day, all week in fact. Why, if you planned this?"

"I didn't lead you on! I had to put up a good performance. You made it clear you didn't want bad publicity."

"And I don't want a tease for a wife."

"I don't want to tease you and I'm not going to be your wife."

"Oh!" Penny should have been warned by the deceptively quiet tone of that single exclamation.

"So this is to be a marriage of convenience is it, little Penny?"

"Yes." His capitulation took all the sting out of her revenge. She'd expected him to protest at least. Now, he drew her towards him, sleek and strong and dangerous. He laughed, a low animal seductive laugh, then drawled: "Won't you miss this, Penny?"

His strength was overpowering. As he pulled her against him, he peeled off the long white robe as if it offended him. She struggled against him but was not proof against the demands in his lean body and the fire in his fingers. She could do nothing as he bent her will to his. His lips, which seared hers with anger and contempt, were nevertheless achingly sweet. Drained by his savage exploring of her body, she allowed herself to drift into a world starred with pleasure. About her body there was a heavy languor and his exultation was fierce with triumph.

"Want me now, Penny?"

The question was cruel, his voice

harsh and abrupt. He did not wait for an answer because her whole body was responding foolishly in a way she could not control. There was no point in fighting any more.

9

PENNY awoke on her own in the single bed she'd chosen on her wedding day. The sheets were tucked tightly round her naked form and, on waking, she wriggled experimently, unused to the aching heaviness in her limbs. She raised herself enough to glance across to the other bed. He was there. He had slept alone as she had intended but not before he'd claimed her as his wife. She flushed to think of the pleasure she had taken in his embrace however forced. If only he'd shown some of the same pleasure, how glad she would have been that he had taken her. Some tenderness would have melted her heart but Chris had been beyond that. What had started in a sneer had ended in triumph and his smile had held that glint of victory. She remembered it now as he'd bent to wrap her in her own bedclothes, not gently as the gesture might imply but possessively.

Now she came suddenly wide awake, aware of her nakedness. Her nightdress was still unpacked and the robe she'd chosen so carefully was lying where Chris had thrown it on the floor. Now he slept as silently as he slept alone. She must dress before he woke. She could not face him like this in the light of the morning. She slid out of bed and edged towards the robe; she would take a bath now to wake herself up. As she stretched up and shook out the crumpled white nylon, a voice said sleepily: "Up at this hour? Couldn't you sleep, little one?"

She snatched the robe closely to her in a vain attempt to cover herself but his laugh was sleepy as he protested:

"Oh, by heaven, not now Penny! I'm still half asleep. Run away and dress, do."

He yawned and stretched lazily, but his eyes did not leave her as she struggled with the robe that enhanced rather than concealed. She grabbed up the underclothes she'd left ready folded and fled to the bathroom, not emerging until she could face him with some dignity. Even then, her colour was high. She had washed even her hair; it was still damp and clung to her head in golden tendrils. She looked very young and his manner was protective as he handed her a cup of tea poured from the pot he'd ordered while she was in the bath.

"I thought we'd have breakfast in here, Penny. In half an hour. That'll give you time to dress before they bring it."

"Thank you."

She was quiet and demure, genuinely touched by his concern for her.

"I'll use the bathroom now, if you don't mind."

"That's all right. I've finished."

"I'll be ten minutes, then."

He left and it was as though he was deliberately giving her time to be alone, to discard the filmy robe and dress again in the dove-grey suit. Tears shimmered in her eyes that this morning he could be so kindly and gentle towards her when last night there had been no word of love or sweet caress to soften his passion. Over breakfast his concern was charming and Penny thought he'd forgotten how she'd meant to use him until he said, "We have to talk, Penny, and it had better be now."

So here was the reckoning! She nodded her assent, unable to trust her voice. Iron bands clamped about her heart and she felt weighed down with sadness. Feeling perhaps, that he'd treated her cruelly Chris seemed to soften before her dewy-eyed look. She was as trusting now as she'd been as a child and he wanted her to stay that way.

"Penny, try to understand. It seems to have upset you unduly that Joanna was at the wedding but, believe me, I didn't invite her. I didn't even see her."

"What was she doing there then?"

She still couldn't forget that humiliation as Joanna's mocking eyes had swept over her.

"She must have been doing the spread for her magazine."

"Spread?"

"Yes. I told you there'd be publicity and Joanna's always handled my publicity before."

"I see. Is that why she looked so pleased with herself?"

"She was probably pleased with the picture you made. You really were breathtakingly beautiful when you came into church."

"And that pleased her?"

"The picture pleased her, I'm sure. She's a perfectionist in her work. That's why we work so much together."

"You take her with you always?"

"Penny, why do you torture yourself so much about who I used to take with me? My bachelor days are over now. I chose to settle down so you must help me to adjust to family life."

"Family life?"

"Yes, Penny, a family. That's what I said. I want daughters to beguile me with that same innocent gaze you can never lose and sons to win their spurs heroically."

This was too much for Penny. The hot tears spilled over her lashes and, sitting still and silent with her hands folded in her lap, she wept.

"Don't weep, my little one. Only trust me. It's going to be all right."

"But."

"No buts, Penny." His tone was quite stern now. "We must both make sacrifices. You must promise never to see Gerald again and I'll have to try to make the same promise about Joanna."

"Only try?"

"It won't be easy. Business will suffer. But I'll do it, Penny. If you insist, I'll arrange not to meet Joanna again."

"Thank you, Chris."

"And you?"

"What about me?"

"Are we still to have this hankering after Gerald? Must I rape my own wife every time I want her?"

Penny longed to cry out that Gerald no longer mattered to her, to declare her love for Chris. If only he would say he loved her, she'd be so glad to fall into his arms.

"Well, Penny?"

"I — I'll try to make you a good wife, Chris, one you can be proud of and a m-mother of those children you want."

"Then why the tears?" he asked gently, so gently that she was overwhelmed and sobbed without restraint. All the tension of the previous weeks poured from her and, although Chris held her and pacified her, she could tell from his face that he was perplexed and hurt.

She was calm again long before they needed to leave for the airport and spent nearly an hour repairing the ravages to her face. The outburst had calmed her and now she managed to drape the velvet into a bright turban of cherry over her smooth hair. Chris came back into the room as she adjusted its folds and he smiled encouragingly at her reflection.

"You look as perky as our little robin, my Penny."

"Pert and bright? I'm glad I look like that."

"You'll need a smile. I'm afraid the photographers are out again."

"Oh, no! Are you so famous?"

"They'll forget us after today. Just smile for them and they'll be happy."

So they left the hotel hand in hand and smiling into the cameras. In the taxi Chris kept a tight hold of her hand. He wasn't romantic in manner but comforting and so he continued throughout the journey, overwhelming her with the gentle consideration his love-making had lacked.

It was a fine spring morning in London when they set out for Spain, a day of white clouds and blue skies. Penny's spirits rose at last, for she was on her way to a country she had never visited and she had visions of warmth and hot sun. The run to the airport was cold though, colder than the bright sun suggested, so that by the time they were aboard the plane Penny had consumed too much hot sweet coffee. She felt slightly nauseated before the flight began and, as it continued, unease with flying together with that sensation of sickness, made the journey an ordeal. Chris, who used the airlines frequently for business transactions, was tireless and kept up a patter of amusing stories for her entertainment. She was too weary to listen and, sensing her need for silence, he fell quiet, watching her as she let the vast panorama of earth move around her unseen. Her face was palely luminous beneath the turban she'd donned for gaiety. The bright cherry tones heightened rather than relieved the pallor of her skin. She looked younger and softer than yesterday and the droop of her lips was pathetically childish. He began to feel a cad for having caused so much of her present languor. He should have waited. There was plenty of time for them. The long lashes making inky crescents on her white face alarmed him. She was still so vulnerable, he was thinking, so untouched. Untouched! If only he could believe that. And yet, despite Gerald, she had preserved that innocent bloom, that out-of-this-world look which tore at his heart.

They drove away from the airport with Chris at the wheel of a car that had been waiting there for them. Everything was organised and travelling with him was smooth. Penny expected a brief journey to a modern hotel but she was mistaken. Chris drove fast and well, threading his way skilfully through the traffic until they were out on a country road, smiling after the spring rain. They passed through green farmland and over arid plains and the sun grew hotter. Chris discarded his jacket and rolled up his shirt sleeves, but Penny could do nothing to relieve the trickles of heat that formed all over her. There was no blouse beneath her suit so she had to stay in the jacket. She undid the top buttons but it wasn't enough. She made a fan out of a paper bag from her overnight case and waved it about, seeking to make some air. The effort was too much for her. She lay back in her seat breathing deeply, praying that she wouldn't disgrace herself now. She didn't notice the new whiteness the towns acquired, the red gleam on the soil or the abundance of trees as they neared their destination. She was too tired to care where they were going.

When they pulled up under the shade of some ilex-trees in front of a farmhouse she did not care that they were watched curiously by a row of dark-skinned, barefoot children. Chris, jumping out, spoke to them with a wide grin and they laughed in reply before scattering towards a group of low white buildings in the distance. Chris came round to open her door. She tried to climb out 'with dignity but her cramped limbs betrayed her.

She stumbled and would have fallen if he had not caught her.

"Careful, little one, you are numb from the journey."

"I'm all right now," she tried to assure him but the ground began to swim in a haze of heat. She leaned against the strength of the arms supporting her and, suddenly, he swept her up and carried her into the farmhouse whispering:

"This, at least, is as it should be."

Chris seemed to know his way about in the house and he carried her straight into a huge kitchen with a floor of stone pavings. He set her down in a chair and brought her a glass of some liquid that was standing covered in a jug on the heavy ugly table in the middle of the room. It tasted vaguely like fruit cup and, finding it refreshing, Penny drank thirstily. Too thirstily, for the room swam, a depressing roundabout of wooden furniture, onions and smoked hams. It was hot and close and she couldn't imagine why Chris had stopped at such a place. He was carrying in her cases. No! Surely not! This couldn't be the place he'd chosen for their honeymoon. Not here, in this primitive farmhouse with nobody for company and nothing to do! Tired, sick and utterly dismayed, she sank her head into her hands in despair. Seeing this, Chris gathered her into his arms again and carried her upstairs. Without a word, he took off her shoes then helped her out of the crumpled grey suit. The huge bed was spotlessly clean and she was pleased to lie down. She was drifting into sleep even as Chris brought a bowl of cold water and a sponge and began to sponge the sweat from her face and down her neck to her shoulders. She barely felt the sheet touch her as he drew it up and left her to sleep. She slept until late evening when she woke to the noise of Chris adjusting the slatted blinds at the window and drawing the curtains. Minutes after that, he was standing beside her with coffee.

"Drink it, Penny," he said and waited until she'd drained the final drop before adding "Would you like to eat now?"

"I'd like a bath first. Is that possible?"

"Yes, of course," he said stiffly, then added, "Penny, I know this isn't what you expected. I'm sorry. I really thought you'd enjoy the Spanish country as much as the English. This farmhouse belongs to a friend. I often stay here in one of the guest-rooms. But the family who keep it, Juan's head man, moved out for us specially."

"Moved out?"

"Yes, down to the buildings you saw below the farm when we drove in."

"You mean we've turned them out of their home?"

"Well, they often move out in the summer and let the house to tourists. Maria comes across to clean and cook. I thought it would be ideal for us."

"Why?"

The one word was more abrupt than she'd meant and he recoiled.

"I thought you'd like the sense of real Spain and, traditionally, honeymoons are meant to be spent alone. Here, there would have been no one to bother us, only Maria and the children."

"Would have been?"

"Yes, we'll move on tomorrow. Don't bother to unpack. It's only the night, Penny. Tomorrow we'll do it all properly."

"Properly?"

"Hotels, apartments, the lot. I promise you a honeymoon to your liking. The accommodation here's a bit primitive, but perhaps you can endure it for one night."

"Of course." Penny was already beginning to like the big room with its sparse furniture and the high old-fashioned bed.

"Hurry, then. I'll show you where to go. Don't linger in the bath because I'm starving."

"So am I," she surprised herself by stating.

"Good. Shall we eat in here or will

you come down to the kitchen?"

"The kitchen, please."

"You sound quite eager," he grinned and Penny was amazed how keen she was to eat when, later, dressed in fresh clothes from her case, she sat at the big table and watched Chris carry dishes over from the charcoal stove where Maria had done the cooking earlier. The food was excellent and the wine went slightly to her head giving her a boldness that made her long for the night. She felt exhilarated as though her sleep had washed away all her doubts and tiredness. Openly she flirted with her husband, leading him on until they stood again in her bedroom, their room. Impulsively, she moved towards him palpitatingly aware of his nearness. His arms closed naturally around her and he kissed her, his lips soft and lingering but without passion. In that moment she became girlishly shy because of the deep serenity that kiss engendered. Now existed something she had not known before, a quiet peaceful happiness that she knew was love. She longed to wind her arms round his neck and tell him but he was already putting her from him. His arms fell to his sides and he stood motionless regarding her for a long moment.

"Penny, little one, this room is yours for tonight."

"What, Chris?" She looked full at him but his glance was deliberately averted. When he did turn, he caught her gaze and held it until she lowered her eyes.

"It's been a long journey for you, Penny, with a disappointing ending. You're tired . . . you're strung up. So, goodnight, little one."

He stepped towards her and lightly kissed her brow. In a panic to keep him with her, Penny asked, "But you, Chris? Where will you sleep?"

"There's the guest-room I always use when I stay here. It'll be ready."

"Where is it?"

"Why, Penny! I do declare you're afraid! Shall I sleep at the foot of your bed like a good knight?"

Immediately she felt silly and let him collect his things in silence. He did not look her way again but made for the door.

"Chris!" She spoke impulsively and he turned instantly, his eyes eager and warm as she looked up to see them.

"Yes?" he asked, his tone giving her no help in what she wanted to say.

"Chris, I'm not a child — far from it."

"I know," he said softly and meaningfully so that a pink flush rose in her cheeks and flooded her face and neck.

"What I mean is — I'm grown up. I understand that you're a man and not an icicle."

"I'm glad you understand that." The eagerness had gone now. He was cool and his tone was one of acceptance rather than desire. "Because I do intend us to have a full marriage."

"Of course." In her shyness she said it stiffly not glancing up and, when he didn't respond, she cried despairingly, "I'll keep my side of the bargain, never fear."

"Bargain!" He said it so faintly that she wasn't sure that was what he said, but when she did bring herself to look up he had gone. She could hear him opening another door and then moving around. She undressed and carefully donned a nylon nightdress and long silk negligée. Her hair was brushed into folds of golden silk over her shoulders but he did not come back. Eventually, she took off the negligée and got into bed, snapping out the light in the hope that he would hear it. His light clicked in reply. Tremblingly she lay there, a quiver of anticipation, but she had no wiles with which to lure him to her bed and she could never tell him of her newly discovered love. Not this Chris who had married her because it was time to create a new image, to establish himself, and who had enjoyed the passion of another woman.

She felt she would never sleep

but eventually she awoke to hear a babble of voices beneath her window as Maria arrived to cook breakfast. Quickly she jumped out of bed and ran to the window. She opened the curtains and drew up the blinds. The children delighted her as they romped on the soft green under the trees, their brown limbs tumbling in a game of their own. Suddenly, one of them became aware of her watching and the whole brood stopped to stare up at her, their liquid eyes gazing curiously at her lightly clad fairness. Penny called to them that she'd be down and hurried back into the room to dress. They didn't understand but she heard their laughter and felt a bond with them. She chose a plain shift of a dress in citrus yellow and caught her hair into a childish pony-tail. Sandals were quickly found so that, within minutes, she was outside and sharing the bench under the ilex-trees with a scrambling heap of brown bodies. A small barefooted girl proudly carried her a glass of fruit juice and Penny knew that Maria must have watched her join the children. Emboldened by her willingness to share their seat, the little ones gathered around her, babbling excitedly and touching her dress, her sandals and then, very tentatively, her hair. A tiny scrap, hardly more than a baby, crawled across her lap so she settled him in her arms from where his fingers stretched out to explore her face.

"You make a charming picture, Penny Precious," said a low voice and there was Chris looking vibrant with life and energy in his casual dress of sweater and slacks. He dropped a kiss on her head as all the little ones except the baby scattered like wild birds. This youngest had cuddled into her arms asleep. Maria herself brought them coffee and carried off the sleeping infant.

Watching her brush down her dress where the child had crumpled it, Chris said, "Perhaps next year it'll be our own baby you'll be holding."

"I hope so," she said then blushed ridiculously, disturbed by the expression in his eyes. Abruptly his manner changed as he remembered the evening before and her protested disgust at their farmhouse accommodation.

"When can you be ready to leave, Penny?" he asked.

"Leave?"

"Yes, we must find a hotel early if we're to find one to your liking."

She bent her head, acutely embarrassed at having to eat her own words.

"Chris, could we go on a picnic?"

"From here?"

"Yes. Is it far to the coast?"

"Not at all. That's part of its charm, for me at any rate."

"Please, Chris?"

"And the hotel?"

"Can we forget it? I'm sorry, Chris. I was overtired yesterday and everything seemed wrong."

"I know, little one." His voice was gentle. "I told you so last night."

The full implication of that left her speechless, but she was so glad of the chance to stay that she jumped up and gave him a quick kiss of gratitude.

"Mmmmm!" he exclaimed appreciatively. "Perhaps I should beat you more often!"

"Chauvinist pig!" she retaliated and they went into breakfast hand in hand, laughing happily.

Their light-hearted banter set the tone for the day and, with Chris in this mood, Penny felt young and even carefree again. He was the Chris of summers long ago, his sense of fun bubbling into the charming mixture of deference and flattery he reserved for her. They started straight after breakfast with Chris driving the car he'd picked up at the airport the day before. It was still early enough for a light mist to be covering the marshy ground and Chris pointed out birds that had their refuge there. All his conversation was light and pleasant, as cool as the freshness of this Spanish morning which would soon be exposed to the relentless rays of a blistering sun. Penny was captivated by the wild flowers that grew by the roadside though Chris pointed out that they were already beginning to wilt. There were hills now running down to the sea and Penny could see vast vineyards and olive groves that occupied the Spaniards of this area. Their white houses were clustered in villages and the red-tiled roofs burned in the growing heat.

When they arrived at the sandy beach Chris had chosen they drove down a narrow track to a deserted cove. It was so perfect with its honey-gold sand and a scattering of rocks that Penny knew he must have visited it before. This was no chance visit. The whole coastline shimmered gold in the sun and, so early in the season, there were comparatively few tourists about. Penny began to realise how carefully he must have planned this honeymoon she'd despised. Her reaction must have shattered him. But his manner showed no sign of disappointment as he parked in the shade of a sandstone hill alongside the path.

"Would you like to bathe?" he grinned.

"Well, yes." She hesitated. "Is that what you want to do?"

"Swim and sunbathe, then enjoy the solitude. We're here and we've got all day."

"But I haven't brought a swimsuit."

"Then we can swim without." His almost animal glance teased her ready blushes. "We'll be children of nature."

"In Spain?"

"Well, yes. What a pity! This is Spain and we should offend those Spanish susceptibilities."

"I'll just sunbathe while you swim."

"Oh, no, you won't! I've got your swimsuit. It's in the boot." It was indeed. He'd brought one of the costumes she'd chosen with such care for this honeymoon, a towel and the beach wrap that was new and gay.

He was dressed and scrambling over

the rocks to the stretch of sand before she could recover from her surprise. Copper-hued shoulders atop a muscled chest tapered to a narrow waist and slim hips. Not sure whether it was tact or eagerness to try the water that made him splash so quickly into the sea, Penny watched his bobbing head disappear. He was an excellent swimmer. She would have liked to go on watching him as he swam under water then surfaced some distance away, but in case he came back for her she undressed quickly behind a massive rock. She would have felt more equal to coping with him in her clothes, but he was already emerging from that silver shimmer where sand melted into sea, thick hair clinging wetly to his forehead and eyes sparkling with enjoyment.

"Come on, shy little Penny," he invited. "The water's fine." Tiny droplets splashed down his bronzed torso as he strode back to her.

"I'm afraid you'll be disappointed in me," she stammered doubtfully, glancing at him shyly. But there was no ardour in his eyes as they flicked appreciatively over her slight figure.

"Never!"

"But — But I can't swim."

Suddenly he threw back his head and laughed out loud.

"Oh, Penny! Little Penny! What a fool you are!"

"I'm sorry, Chris. I just can't."

For a moment, his gaze was dark and unfathomable but then he said, "Don't worry. Just relax, my Penny, and leave it all to me. I'll teach you."

She was trembling as he took her hand to lead her over the rocks and she cried out as she slipped and would have fallen but for his arms. She found herself swept up into the air. He held her easily and continued leaping from rock to rock as she clung to him closely.

"I can walk, you know," she assured him.

"I promised to look after you. Don't rob me of my pleasures, little Penny."

Once in the buoyant water she found it less frightening than she'd anticipated. Chris was a good teacher and, before long, the reserve between them had gone and they laughed and splashed happily. Soon she was able to manage a few strokes while he held her chin. Success went to her head. She struck out alone then panicked and felt herself sinking. She clutched at Chris only to be guided back to the shallows. When he told her she had been in long enough for the first time, she felt unreasonably disappointed. She towelled herself vigorously, then lay back in the sun. She began to feel drowsy. Soon her eyes became so heavy, the sun so warm upon her skin, that she felt herself drifting into sleep. She roused with a start. The sun was lost in the shadow of Chris bending over her. He was dressed.

"Come on, Penny! No more sleep. Time to move on."

"Oh! It's so lovely here."

"Yes, but I know a place where it's

high and yet sheltered — a perfect place for lunch."

"Mmmmm. I am hungry. Are you?"

"So hungry I'll eat you if you don't get dressed."

She hurried to comply while he fetched the picnic basket from the car.

"We'll walk a little, carry the picnic," he told her. They did and when they emerged into a clearing some time later she caught her breath at the wonder of the view. They were high on a rocky shelf and suspended over the sea which broke silently a thousand feet beneath them. Chris was studying her entranced features as he asked:

"You like it?"

"It's lovely!" she sighed. "Why can't one always be happy?"

"I suppose one has to earn the right to be happy," he replied. "But what's stopping you now?"

"Today yes, but tomorrow? One is never happy tomorrow."

"Penny, this is now. All life is now. Be happy in it."

"Yes, Chris. Today, I am happy."

"And that's enough. Let's eat now before the wine gets too warm."

They ate prawns first, and they were delicious. Then they had chicken with a loaf of bread, cheese, tomatoes and olives. After the meal, they washed in a hill stream before Chris suggested some sightseeing for the afternoon. Later, they wandered down cobbled streets and saw the sights as other tourists did. They ate again and drove home across the darkening plain to a house left ready by Maria. Everything was fresh and clean and there was food waiting for them on the old-fashioned stove. Penny bathed, then dressed while Chris took a shower. She felt relaxed in the wide trousered leisure pyjamas she'd brought for casual wear. Chris, though, was more formal in a suit, his daytime gaiety having given way to a brooding silence. He was quiet throughout the meal, though he attended to her every need. When they'd finished and she stated her intention of retiring to bed, he stood outside and, from the bedroom window, she could see his dark shadow under the ilex-trees.

She knew that he would come to her tonight and prayed that it would be in the loving mood of the day. But there was so much bitterness in him. He must have been badly hurt by Joanna's rejection and had married Penny thinking his injured vanity would be soothed by her compliance. What had she done? She'd flaunted Gerald in his face, let Chris think she'd run to him only days before their wedding. Impossible now to make him believe in her innocence.

Impossible to give him back his pride. She made ready for his coming with care, stressing her look of innocence yet reclining on the huge bed in a way that was suggestive and inviting. Looking down on her, he laughed harshly.

"I could almost convince myself that you love me!" She whispered, "Chris, I do."

"Not as I want to be loved, not

with another man's name on your lips. You women are all alike, out to use a man."

She wanted to strike back, to salvage the remnants of her own pride with cruel words, but he gave her no time. With a swift movement he reached for her, pulling her up from the bed into his arms and instinctively her own arms went round his neck. His hands bruised her, his lips ravished her, but she felt no pain only rapture. She was utterly his but he was too intent on his own revenge to notice the sweetness of her surrender. He made the night beautiful for her but with a beauty that was washed with tears. And in the morning his tenderness re-made her.

So it was to be. By day a charming companion full of tender concern and playful laughter but by night the dominant male. Never did the two meet. The days were an enduring enchantment for Penny, but by night she suffered humiliation and hurt because of what appeared to be his contempt for her. This husband who could be so kindly and full of friendship offered her no single friendly glance, no caress, no gentleness when he possessed her person. Equally, her daytime companion never made an advance, not a hint of flirtation. Yet, despite his arrogant treatment of her, she always yielded and the more she yielded the more he made her his for ever. She woke each day to the pleasure of his company. He strove to build that innocence which once he'd loved in Penny. In bed, he hungered to annihilate it. This was the tenor of their honeymoon, for Penny a turmoil of alternating shame and entrancing pleasure. Her shame was not that he took her but that he appeared to hate himself for doing so. She longed for his love but he seemed to hate her so.

They stayed at the farmhouse for two weeks, two weeks of bliss and despair, then they spent a week moving from one hotel to another seeing a different side of Spain. This week was an extension of their honeymoon because Chris had business associates to meet. They were wined and dined like celebrities and by day there was shopping and sightseeing. Chris was generous and Penny strove to be the wife he'd be proud of. In Spain, her blonde, blue-eyed beauty could hardly fail. Chris was the envy of the dark young men who clamoured for his custom and their wives cast side-long glances at the girl who could cause such a stir yet remain coolly unaware of the ripples. They could have stayed another month and still not coped with all the invitations that were showered upon them. As it was, they had to return to England. Chris was needed and Penny was anxious to get to grips with the Cottage Hotel. Summer was only a warmth of grass away when they returned to Grange House. To the villagers who saw them arrive the young couple were radiant.

10

MOLLY, Chris's housekeeper, greeted them with warmth. Penny had always been slightly in awe of the gaunt grey-haired woman who ran Grange House so efficiently. Now, though, the older woman showed her the deference a new mistress might expect without unbending into servitude. To Chris she was as motherly as ever, inquiring after his well-being and grumbling slightly that he was late. She had prepared lunch for them and it had been ready for an hour. Hurrying upstairs to wash and freshen up, Chris and Penny were conspiratorial in their endeavours to please her with their promptness. Instead of being rather strange lunching together for the first time in their new home, it was gay in the sunny dining-room being waited on by Molly. She insisted that every crumb was finished and would not hear of slimming diets or fads, though Chris teased Penny about losing her figure to Molly's cooking.

Upstairs in their room after the meal, the afternoon yawned before Penny. Chris had driven off with barely a muttered excuse after the honeymoon had taught her to expect his presence. She was not used to having time on her hands or to being alone. Feeling a sudden desire to see her parents she went downstairs and out on the wide lawns. Still lingering in her mind was the picture of Chris's eyes gleaming at her in humour across the table as he teased Molly. A curious light-hearted feeling spurred her on as she set off down the drive. She was wearing sandals and the soft verges were kind to her feet as she strolled towards the village. She was in no hurry this afternoon. The sun was shining and the village was alive with all its usual daily tasks. It was good just walking and soaking up the sights of home.

Her mother was delighted to see her. Penny had brought her some new cologne and a satchet of petit-point handkerchiefs which she'd found in a little embroidery shop in Spain. There was wine for her father but it had been too heavy for her to carry today.

"I'll get Chris to drop it in," she told her parents as they sat drinking tea in the cool of the kitchen. "He chose it when we visited some wine cellars last week."

"You went visiting, then?" her mother inquired.

"Well, that was business really."

"What, tasting wine!" her father joked.

"Not exactly. Chris says you have to get acquainted with the people who matter to get what you want in business."

"And that means entertaining?"

"Yes, in a big way."

"We shan't see much of you, then?" her father asked wistfully. Before she could reply an unmistakable voice called:

"Is my wife here?"

"Chris! What are you doing here?" Penny jumped up and ran to the door to let him in. He ruffled her hair playfully and asked, "Why did you disappear like that?"

"Me disappear? Why, Chris, you went off and left me alone so I came over here."

"Running home to mother, already?" The teasing light in his eyes softened the remark and she took his hand and pulled him through to the kitchen where her parents welcomed him warmly. There was an air of suppressed excitement about him and, refusing tea, he burst out, "Come and see what I've got for you."

"For me?"

"Yes. Come on. I couldn't wait to bring it home to you and then you were out. Even Molly didn't know where you were."

As he spoke he was urging her out to the road where a primrose yellow Mini was parked. "There you are.

All yours. Like it?"

"Oh, Chris!" In her gratitude she caught his hand and held it tightly. Her shining eyes seemed to dazzle him.

"But it's fabulous Chris. I'm almost speechless."

He smiled. He pressed her fingers entwined in his and looked down at their clasped hands. Abruptly, he released them and said, "You'll need the car. You're going to be very busy at the hotel and sometimes I'll need you to drive up to London."

"Oh!"

"You'll have to help me with the entertaining. Now I'm a married man, it'll be expected."

"But surely that will be at Grange House?"

"Some of it, yes. But there are always business lunches and dinners in town."

"And you'll want me?"

"You're my wife, aren't you?"

"Oh Chris — how can I ever thank you?"

He looked down into her animated face. "In the usual fashion. Not here. At home."

She coloured deeply and scrambled inside the car to inspect the interior. Her mother and father came out to see the Mini and there was much light-hearted banter about the lavish wedding present before they drove back to Grange House with Penny behind the wheel of her own car. They drove with a warm silence between them. Penny thought he'd forgotten her thank you. But he hadn't. He came out of his dressing-room when they were changing for dinner and crossed the wide expanse of their bedroom to where she stood. Aware of her scanty turquoise slip, she turned crimson with embarrassment. "Chris! I didn't expect — "

"I came for the 'thank you' you promised me." It was the first time he had come to her in daylight. He could see her eyes were wide in shyness. "Come on, I'm waiting. All night if necessary."

"But Chris, I — " She stopped, stretched up timidly and put her lips to his cheek.

"Penny! You can do better than that."

He took her arms one by one and placed them round his neck. "Keep them there." His arms came round her waist. "Go on!"

"Thank you, Chris, for my lovely car."

Slowly, her mouth approached his and she closed her eyes as she kissed him. Now, she had to convince him of her love. She was engulfed by a desire to submit unreservedly to his demands. As his passion increased, she clung to him, yielding to the mastery of his lips and the caressing of his hands.

"My word!" he said, breathing heavily, "if you can respond like that, no wonder Gerald came back for more."

Her hand swung upwards but before it made contact with his cheek he deftly caught her wrist and gripped it cruelly.

Tears swamped her eyes and she was choked with anger. "Who do you think I am?"

"My wife, and I have greater claim on you than anyone else. Why should I deny myself the pleasure of you?"

She was helpless in his grip of iron as she pleaded. "But Chris, I was trying to thank you in the way you wanted."

"Yes. Begging for my attentions!"

"That's not fair!"

"Well, if it's warmth and passion you want, I've got enough to lavish on the likes of you."

He jerked her against him and his mouth came down savage and merciless. He pressed her backwards and down on to the bed and a sensation of intense joy took possession of her. She was back where she truly belonged. She was powerless to resist his urgency.

Afterwards he didn't turn away from her or leave her. It was she who rolled away and closed her eyes. When she did find sufficient courage to look at him, he was gazing at her with an expression she hadn't seen in his eyes before. Her heart raced.

"I think it's time we got ready for dinner, don't you?" He smiled, stood up and held out his hand to her.

"Coming?"

She nodded and his lips pressed against her hair.

"Penny, you're an enigma. At times you seem so innocent and yet — "

He turned and strode back to his dressing-room, but he didn't close the door and he was back to zip her into the coffee-coloured dress she'd chosen for dinner. As they went down to the dining-room, his arm slipped round her and, to Molly who was waiting to serve, they looked most convincing especially when Chris's cheek rubbed against her hair. After the meal, sitting by his side in the circle of his arm she felt she could not ask for more. They listened to records until Penny was overcome with yawns. She tried to stifle them because she did not want to break the magic spell. But Chris had noticed and asked her if she wanted to go to bed. She nodded and he pulled her from the couch. His hand grasped hers as they walked towards the stairs.

She was in bed and nearly asleep when he came out of his dressing-room wearing a short towelling robe over his pyjamas. He sat on the edge of her bed and hesitated before saying, "Penny, I owe you a profound apology for the way I treated you tonight."

"But, Chris, it's where I belong — in your arms."

"Yes, but not in the way I've taken you in these last weeks. Can you forgive me, Penny?"

"There's nothing to forgive, Chris."

He dropped a kiss on her forehead. "Penny, I've got to be up early. I'm going into town. Do you want to come?"

"Why?"

"We could have lunch together and you could go and spend some money on new gowns."

"Is that necessary?"

"Well, my sweet, we'll be entertaining on a lavish scale soon and you'll need some new models."

"More?"

"Yes, more. I want everyone to see how beautiful my wife is."

"Thank you."

"That's settled then. I'll bring you tea and we'll make an early start. Goodnight, Penny."

"Goodnight?"

"Yes, we have to be up early and you're tired. Go to sleep now. Never mind, there's always tomorrow."

He bent to kiss her and she curled her arms around his neck. Their kiss seemed never ending. Tears were in her eyes when they parted.

"Real ones?" he whispered as he touched them with his finger. She longed to cry out that there would be no tears if only he'd stay, but she had no voice. He pulled the covers over her as though she were a child. She looked up and smiled her thanks and his smile in return was the sweetest she had ever seen.

The next day set a kind of pattern for Penny. She enjoyed the fitting sessions and, half in love with the woman cool and poised who smiled back at her from the mirrors, she blossomed in confidence. She didn't stop at evening wear but found herself trying on elegant summer suits and afternoon dresses. When she was wearing a salmon-coloured suit with a striped scarf at the throat, her assistant smiled and complimented her:

"That is just right for madam's colouring. Unusual, but lovely."

"I'll keep it on," Penny said, agreeing with the girl and immediately matching shoes were supplied to complete the outfit. She ran down the steps of the fashion house, secure in the knowledge that she looked her best. She had no idea how long Chris had been waiting outside in his car, but he looked content and his eyes lit up to see her.

"How about some lunch?" he asked

as he gathered up the papers he had been busy with and she took her place beside him. Penny had no idea where they were going to find a meal in this part of the city amid the rush of business life but Chris appeared to have something in mind. He manoeuvred his way skilfully through the traffic to an area of narrow streets. Then, leaving the car in a secluded lane, he led her to an unobtrusive doorway. Penny followed him into what seemed to be a refuge for successful businessmen. She felt ridiculously shy for a moment, but then relaxed to form with Chris a picture of ease at one of the alcove tables. The food was appetising and Penny found the whole experience most enjoyable.

Towards the middle of the meal, Chris asked, "Any more to do this afternoon?"

"Never! I've spent far too much already!"

"Would you like to go to the zoo or something?"

"The zoo? But why?"

"We've been invited out to dinner tonight. Could you stay in town and join me later?"

"Yes — I can rescue one of the outfits I bought this morning if I dash back before they pack it all."

"I'll drive you there after lunch. It's the afternoon I'm worried about. My secretary has booked us a room at the hotel where we're dining so you can go there as soon as you like."

"Are we staying the night, then?"

"I don't think so, but you'll need somewhere to change and I shall want to relax before the meal. But I don't want you to mope about in a hotel room all afternoon."

"But, Chris, I've got so much to do! I can go and look at window drapes for the cottage and I'd like to find a huge old refectory table to stand in the reception area. And — "

"Hold your horses, Penny! I get the message. You'll be quite happy to browse on your own. But, please don't overdo it."

Suddenly, their conversation came alive. Penny was excited by the opportunity to consider curtain material and wall décor, a subject which Chris discussed as enthusiastically as she did herself. It was after two before they emerged into the sunshine and they had to get back to the fashion house quickly. Chris dealt with the question of rescuing an evening dress from her morning's selection. A few words with a dapper little man quickly brought the black tailored girl who had helped her so much. She carried some of the house's delicate creations into the office where they waited and Chris immediately asked for a white flowing dress with silver encircling the throat to be sent to his hotel. Penny checked with the girl that all the necessary accessories would be with it, even down to a diamante clip for her hair. She would have to find the right make-up during the afternoon.

It wasn't until she was in the bath

much later that she realised she'd forgotten the make-up. Her afternoon had been so busy. She hadn't had time to miss Chris. The shops had been closing their doors before she'd taken a taxi to the address Chris had given her. He had been in and showered before her so she hurried to take her bath and be ready for him. When she confessed about the make-up, he merely laughed and said, "With your Spanish tan you won't need it."

Sure enough, the soft tan on her cheeks needed only a dusting from her own compact to give it a peach-coloured bloom against the white dress and her soft rose lipstick was all the colour she needed. The evening was a great success and they drove home together long after midnight in contented silence.

Often, after that, Penny spent a day in London with Chris or sometimes he would ring her and she'd drive up in the Mini to have dinner with him and his associates. She became popular with the men he entertained and he became lazily confident of her success. Beneath his flattering smile and the toasts of the company's directors Penny opened up like a flower in the sun. She smiled at their remarks and listened with a sympathetic ear and always had a fund of stories to cover the embarrassing gaps in conversation. Most of these stories — amusing in the main — centred on her attempts to get the Cottage Hotel ready for opening. On the days Chris didn't need her she devoted all her energies to the renovations. She was kept busy at the cottage for the best part of each day, arriving back at Grange House just before Chris in the evenings. Always she was there to greet him, cool and lovely in her light summer dresses, to have a drink with him and to share the meal that Molly prepared. He was always eager to hear of her day and her progress and she enjoyed telling him everything. It gave her great satisfaction to see the rooms at the cottage taking shape. As often as she could she would take Chris down to stroll with her through the scenes she was creating. He didn't say a lot but she knew that he approved and a faint glow of pride filled her.

She allocated rooms according to the staff requirements and instructed hired helpers on where and how to arrange the new furniture as it arrived. She found that she enjoyed being at the head of a team instead of merely a part of the bustling activity. This time she appointed a chef, a tall, thin individual who would require sleeping accommodation on the premises. Also Ted and June would live in at the hotel, occupying a flat built on at the side together with other new rooms she'd needed. The couple had worked out a month's notice with Gerald under trying circumstances as Penny was to learn later and then returned to London to be married in the registry office of the London borough where June had been born. Chris and Penny were invited and to the celebratory lunch after the ceremony. Penny was surprised that Chris insisted on going. She hadn't expected weddings to be much in his line. There were no parents, only another couple as well as Penny and Chris. The room was gay enough with flowers, the bride was pretty and the service almost the same but, to Penny, the whole scene lacked atmosphere. Remembering her own wedding she reflected on how lucky she was and, catching Chris's gaze on her, let her smile show her feelings. She was glad that later, over lunch, he got on well with the couple she'd chosen to run her hotel.

After their honeymoon, Ted and June moved in and, suddenly, the cottage was ready. Penny had devoted every spare moment to it but now she could take a back seat. All that remained for her was to organise the opening. She needed to create an occasion for that and, funnily enough, it rose out of her success in Chris's world. They were having drinks with some important officials of his company and discussing a house-party to be held at Grange House when one of the men lifted his glass to Penny above the din of the room and said, "No doubt, your husband owes his recent success in the company to you, my dear."

All the men's attention was focused on Penny, who felt herself blush deeply. Chris took a drink from his glass and then added to her embarrassment by outlining her own venture at the cottage. The big man who had spoken first now turned his roguish glance to Penny.

"And when can we see this country-hotel you've created?" The idea hit her immediately and she blurted out, "Well, why don't you hold your house-party there? It would make a fantastic opening."

"This wife of yours certainly knows how to go for the big business, Chris! How much would such a caper cost the company?"

Appalled at having wrested the

house-party from Grange House as a business venture for the Cottage Hotel, Penny stuttered, "B-But Chris, I-I didn't mean it like that."

"Of course you did!" rang out the infectious laugh of the big man and his rascally gaze tormented Penny again.

"You arrange the financial details with your wife, Chris, then fix the publicity."

"Publicity?"

"Yes, Mrs. Lloyd. Publicity will help your hotel and it certainly won't do our company any harm."

Would he invite Joanna, then? As if sensing her thoughts, Chris moved closer to her and smiled his congratulations at her conquest. She was pleased. He may have married her out of pity or to spite Joanna but she had certainly made her mark with his friends. He'd said that his career needed marriage and, in that field, she would not fail him. Lately his entire manner with her was softening. This opening weekend for her hotel must be a time to remember for Chris's friends. She must find out from him who were to be the important guests. Before they left Alderbridge, they'd be eating out of her hand. No, his hand! She must play down her part in the success to boost him.

Her life became a hive of activity in preparation for the visit. Her hostessing role was drawing near and she hadn't the faintest idea how she was going to cope in the staged and moneyed atmosphere of big business. Thank goodness there was plenty to do to take her mind off the worries. With Chris she made a list of the most influential people to be invited and he took it for his secretary to type out the invitations. When he brought these home for her to see she noticed that each message had a personal friendly touch as though he was well acquainted with the people who mattered.

Together, they toured the Cottage, as her venture was now affectionately called, and she made notes as efficiently as she could of all his requests. There were flowers for all the rooms to be ordered for delivery on the Friday in question. The larder had to be stocked, and Penny helped Ted to check the contents of the delivery vans against the chef's lists. Ted had an easy relationship with the elegant young chef who was already a fixture on the premises. It was left to Ted, too, to engage the various temporary house-staff required for the weekend. As the time drew near, Penny learned how to leave more and more to Ted. He and June were often still busy at the end of the day, but Penny never failed to drop everything and go home to Chris. As this new role taught her to delegate so it added stature to Ted's authority. With a wife beside him he combined business with pleasure and the Cottage was his home as much as he was at home in it. They didn't know many people in the village, but they had each other and that seemed to be enough. Now and again, Penny was tempted to invite them up to Grange House for an evening, but she was jealous of Chris's attention and she wanted her marriage to herself. She and Chris had settled into an easy relationship without the bitterness of the early days. True, Penny longed to be the one who held the key to his locked up heart. In the beginning she had envied Joanna with all her soul but now she had settled for what Chris had to give her. He no longer fought to break down her defences, using his lovemaking and his kisses as weapons. Each time he kissed her the ice melted a little so that the stark excruciating jealousy of Joanna merged into the past. When he crushed her to him and his lips sought hers she was lost to the world. At times it seemed that he must love her but she couldn't be sure. She began to observe and analyse every situation, trying to judge dispassionately so that she might arrive at the truth. Sometimes she thought his contentment was that of a man who had found the answer to a tantalising and deeply complex problem, though he was still swift to strong passion that seemed to have its driving force in anger. Those times tore her heart out, but her love never dimmed. She began to tell him of it herself in so many little ways without being able to put it into words. If only he would show her that Joanna was forgotten and that he had a place for her, Penny, in his heart.

On the Friday of the weekend party Penny was at the Cottage early. She had brought all they needed in the Mini because she and Chris had decided it would be more convenient to use a bedroom on the premises than to keep going backwards and forwards to the house. Ted was proud to show her into one of the best rooms where she deftly arranged Chris's suits and her own outfits in the huge wardrobe. Chris was coming down early, but Ted and June had prepared everything so efficiently that Penny still found herself with time on her hands. She felt edgy when she thought of the evening to come. They were lucky with the weather. It was warm and bright, so Penny strolled down into the orchard to find solace. She set off through the trees, seeing these acres as she wanted them to be, a playground to her hotel. Plans for landscaping it formed and re-formed in her mind with little scenes from the past lingering and finding a home in the future garden. It was here that Chris found her later and, somehow, their hands stretched out, touched and held. It seemed so natural at first that they scarcely noticed it. Then Penny became aware of what had happened. For the first time since their marriage Chris had made a loving gesture that had nothing to do with the act of making love. She felt shy as if he were courting her and she looked at him expecting him to pull his hand away, but he didn't. He seemed to have cast away the years that had been between them and they were back in the childhood realm but no longer children. As they strolled he was more relaxed than she had ever known him. His eyes, when they looked at her, held a light that seemed to glow for her alone. Her heart beat faster.

"Let's sit down somewhere, Penny. This week has been hectic and I'm tired out."

They found a seat cunningly placed amongst the thick greenery of the orchard and around it a wide space neatly clipped. They chose the grass, Chris spreading out his coat for her to sit on. Both seemed to have ignored the seat by mutual consent. Penny lay back and let the sound of a lawn-mower in the distance, incessant bird-song and, much nearer, Chris's breathing all merge together. She and Chris were together. She was content. But he hovered over her and she opened her eyes to look directly into his only inches away. The sun glanced down on her catching her profile so that it glowed as clear as a cameo cut from the background of soft grass.

How lovable her face was to him.

It was so soft with a creamy blush to enhance its alabaster paleness. No, there was nothing alabaster about it! It was real, vital and alive. The red of her lips was distracting, infatuating and, as she became aware of his watching her, her tongue tipped the curve of her top lip nervously. That was too much! Slowly, purposefully, his lips descended and for a long ecstatic moment they clung together. Penny was taken by surprise but she yielded to the embrace with an inevitableness that was true happiness. This was really her lover come out of the cover of the nights to claim her in the sunshine. She sank upon him with something very like an ecstatic cry.

He raised his head at last, but only to beg:

"Now you kiss me, Penny. Kiss me, my precious.

She could not resist the urgency in his voice or the light in his eyes. She clasped his neck and her kisses were those of an ardent woman on the lips of one she loved with all her heart and soul.

"Now, my Penny Precious, I have you."

"Does it make you happy to have me? I am already yours. I am your wife."

"Mine for ever and ever, Penny?"

He clasped her close and kissed her.

"Yes!"

She had no sooner said it than the tears welled up in her treacherous eyes.

"Why do you cry, my darling?"

"I don't know, Chris — quite — I am so glad to be yours — so happy!"

"It's a funny way to show it."

"I know, but Chris I am so truly happy — so very happy."

"Penny, do you care for me? Really love me? I wish you could prove it in some way."

"But, Chris, how can I prove it more than I have done?"

"Oh, Penny! Why did I wait? Why

didn't I make you love me when you were only sixteen? If I had only known!"

"Known what Chris? Why are you so bitter in your regret?"

"I should have known your heart if I'd taken you then, so pure and lovely and truly loving."

"But my heart is yours, Chris. Let me show you this weekend." He silenced her with a kiss then stood up. "I think it's time we went, don't you?" He held out his hand to her. "Coming?"

They returned to the cottage hand in hand, Penny's heart bursting with love as her soul whispered within: "Oh my love, my love, why do I love you so when you love another? I could have been that one, perhaps I will be. Please God!"

She said not a word out loud and Chris glanced down to ask, "Who are you dreaming of, Penny?"

"Why?"

"You looked so intense as if longing

for something. Do you still have regrets?"

"No, Chris. No regrets at all."

"What would make you happy, then?"

"To hear the man I love say he loves me."

"The man you love?"

"Yes, Chris."

There, by the door, she looked thoughtfully up at him meeting the appreciation in his eyes. Her love for him, the very breath and life of her whole being, glowed in her eyes. She waited for him to speak, but just then Ted opened the door from the other side and, for the time being, their moment was lost. As she ran upstairs to change, though, the buoyancy of her step was marked, skimming the stairs like a bird about to alight. For the whole weekend, her new-found joy was apparent, the joy of a woman in company with the man she loves. It gave her a radiance that everyone noticed. She walked in brightness.

That evening the cars started to arrive. They parked in the large natural space Penny had cleared from woodland. With its wooded parking spaces, it blended into the countryside yet was convenient and efficient for the guests. The guests started to percolate into the rooms and Penny and Chris were always at the front door to greet each newcomer. There was no awkwardness. Smiling couples were coming in from the night and Penny smiled in reply. Chris was shaking hands and welcoming the flow of people yet never neglecting to introduce Penny and to let his pride in her shine out.

Nothing seemed more natural to her after that than to go on attending to the guests' needs. She helped out wherever she could until everyone had arrived and a hush had settled over the Cottage. She felt the content of a mother who knows the old family rooms to be full again after her children have grown up and left. This was her role. She was fulfilled.

Later, up in her room, she applied a brush of colour to her face to liven up the severity of the black she had chosen to wear. It was a daring gown with long see-through sleeves and a rather low-cut bosom. Chris had gone down before her and she felt vaguely shy at having to go down alone. As she came down the curving staircase, though, he turned as if immediately aware of her and watched her progress. He came to meet her, his gaze locking hers as he slid an arm round her waist.

"My word!" came the gruff laughing voice of Penny's favourite director as he turned his roguish humour on them. "They've got it bad, haven't they?"

"You're green-eyed," quipped Chris, keeping his arm firmly in place.

"True, but I never expected to see you caught."

"I haven't been caught! I'm still a free agent."

"Never!" roared their tormentor so that Chris capitulated.

"All right. All right. I give in. I'm in love and I don't care who knows it."

The assembled company loved it and by their silent appreciation and laughing jokes asked for more.

"Come on, Penny," Chris whispered into her ear during a lull, "Let's give them something worth shouting about!"

She smiled into his eyes. She didn't have to act even if he did. She wanted to tell him that.

"Keep it up, precious. They're loving every minute of it." Together, they moved towards the buffet tables which were filled with delicacies of every kind and Penny drifted towards Ted whose anxious face betrayed a problem. Quickly she settled it and, while he was attending to the wine waiters, she moved in to rescue the big man who uncharacteristically was alone in a corner with no one to talk to. He seemed very taken with Penny and, elderly though he was, he flaunted a kind of gallantry as he chatted to her.

"Keep your eyes off my wife!" Chris called to him as he danced by with someone else. This gave him the idea of dancing and, of course, Penny was his partner. He wasn't a dancing man and, being an extrovert, drew attention to this fact. Everybody laughed and Penny blushed with embarrassment at being the centre of attention. Soon Chris rescued her and held her close to him with his cheek brushing her hair so that she relaxed. It was late when the party broke up. Happy with the way the evening had turned out, the guests drifted away to their rooms. As if in a magic spell, Penny let Chris lead her to their room. She was intoxicated by his declared love, even if he had only pretended.

Dinner on Saturday night was a more formal affair. During the day, the fleet of cars had driven out into the countryside for picnics. Dressed in casual day-clothes, Penny had joined them with Chris. Obviously remembering her cooking expertise at Avon House, he had expected her to stay in the kitchens.

"The meal is all arranged," she explained. "I discussed it with the chef before breakfast this morning."

"So that's where you go to!" he burst out so explosively that Penny blushed to think how reluctantly she'd slipped from his side in the early morning.

"Did you want me?" she asked demurely.

"What a question!"

It was only then that Penny realised her blunder. Her cheeks burned and the big boss coming upon them at that moment turned his full humour on their embarrassment.

For the rest of the day he openly flirted with Penny, leaving his wife and Chris to adopt attitudes of affectionate tolerance.

The weekend ended officially after lunch on Sunday. It was a very special lunch and their guests lingered over it, enjoying the sunny dining-room and the good food. Everyone seemed reluctant to go, and Penny found herself specially employed entertaining the directors' wives while their husbands indulged in last-minute discussions with Chris. At last there was only one to go, the big man puffing on the last of his cigar, his great bulk spilling over the armchair he relaxed in. His wife settled back, amiably content to let the conversation wash over her while she waited. Penny hoped that she made a similar picture of serenity, but she was tense with excitement. She'd done it! No one could say she hadn't been the perfect wife this weekend! She longed to hear that praise on Chris's lips. She'd have to wait because, in the end, he'd escorted the last couple out to their car and they were still deep in conversation. On the pretext of going in search of refreshment she went into the kitchen. She was struck by the jaunty mood that prevailed there. Everybody was in holiday spirit. Ted and June glowed with pride. Obviously, Chris had found time to congratulate them and Ted was brimming with news of reservations for future weekends.

"Will you join us in our celebrations tonight?" he asked Penny, though he did not seem to expect her to accept.

"Celebrations?"

"Haven't you heard?" asked the eager young chef, already preparing another culinary masterpiece. "Your husband was so pleased with the success of the weekend that he arranged for us to serve a special meal for the staff tonight, to celebrate."

Penny was pleased at their high spirits but, feeling suddenly low, she went up to her room. Worn out after the culmination of weeks of preparation, she packed simply because she couldn't bear to sit around. She was still busy when Chris came in.

"Leave that, darling. Let's go home."

Something in his gaze drew her towards him. He put out his arms and she turned blindly in his direction, clinging to him with all her strength.

He held her as if he would never let her go.

"Let's get rid of Molly and shut the door to visitors for the rest of the day," he whispered, his lips trailing along her throat. His intentions were obvious and Penny was overcome with joy.

"Chris. Oh Chris!" she whispered and hid her face against him. It was then that the tension of weeks caught up on her. The world inside her head swam dangerously and Chris's rock-hard chest seemed to be a sliding chasm. She crumpled in his arms as the room swayed and blurred. With a curse he whipped her off her feet and placed her gently on the bed calling for June to come and help him. Between them they got her into bed and rang for a doctor who advised a quiet night and plenty of rest. She'd failed Chris again, but from the line of the doctor's questions she knew that she might soon be able to give him news that would delight him. Why hadn't she pondered the cause of that nausea in the mornings before? She'd put it down to nerves. She couldn't wait to tell Chris but she had to be sure. In the night, lying sleepless, she told herself that Chris had been about to declare his love. Surely, his eyes had been dark with love. Surely, she had found what she was seeking in his face. She was still thinking about it when she at last went to sleep.

11

NEXT morning it was June who brought her breakfast in bed, rousing her from a deep sleep. She was propped up on pillows and fussed over as much as anybody could have wished, but Chris was nowhere to be seen. June said he had left early and Penny didn't like to admit that she hadn't known his plans. Within minutes of settling Penny with her tray. June was back holding a florist's spray. "They've just arrived!" she enthused. "It must be a thank you from one of your admirers this weekend."

But Penny looked at the rich velvety red rosebuds and the chaste lilies of the valley nestling among them and knew that the flowers came from Chris. There was a note which she read again and again after June had gone.

My Penny Precious,

Sorry I had to leave. You looked so angelic sleeping that I hadn't the heart to wake you.

I want to thank you for a fabulous weekend — in the usual fashion. Tonight? Give Molly the evening off and serve champagne in our room.

Until then, this is a token.

CHRIS

A token! A token of what? — his love or his gratitude? It had to be both. She'd rest this morning, since June was so insistent. She couldn't risk another fiasco like last night; tonight had to be perfect.

She was whirled onward through the day in a fast tide of anticipation. Her one desire now was to make herself his in an act of pure love. He was her very own and her love must compel a response. No longer would his face glow down on her angry, bold or full of bitterness — just loving.

More and more flowers arrived during the day, each visit of the florist's van heightening Penny's excitement. All of the weekend guests had sent their compliments in this way and she drove from the Cottage with the little yellow Mini piled high in a confusion of colours. Quixotically, she carried all these flowers into their bedroom, creating a scented bower at which Molly sniffed disapprovingly on entry. She had come to tell Penny she was wanted on the telephone, and Penny ran down to the hall laughing to herself. Chris would share the joke tonight of Molly's outrage at the sumptuous love-nest. Her long pointed features and narrow eyes had clearly held Penny's efforts in disdain. Better to give Molly her time off now and she'd be able to walk over to her sister's before tea leaving Penny to cool the champagne without her arrogant disapproval. Picking up the receiver she spoke gaily into it, expecting Chris or one of their recent guests to reply. With a feeling of faintness she heard Gerald's voice and registered its urgency before she understood his message.

When Molly saw her again, she was so pale that the housekeeper grew anxious. "Can I help you?"

"I don't know, Molly, I just don't know. Everything today had to be perfect, but now this has happened. Why now? Why today? There couldn't have been a worse time."

"What has happened, my dear?"

"A — a friend has died and her husband wants me to go to Devon to help him through the crisis."

"Then you must go."

"But today? Must I go today? Will Chris ever forgive me if I leave today?"

"Of course he will. He's the most understanding man I know. I'll see that he understands for you."

"Will you, Molly? Will you explain? It couldn't be more important that he knows I didn't want to go today, but a life depends on it."

"Oh, you are a dramatic one! Get

away with you now and I'll try to get Mr. Christopher in London for you."

"Oh, yes, Molly!" She ran upstairs more readily at the hope.

"When you get him, I'll take it in the bedroom." But Chris could not be contacted, and Penny had to leave without speaking to him. She left a note but all she could write was:

All day I've been longing and hoping to make you happy.

I thought what joy it would be to be a perfect wife.

Please forgive me,

PENNY

She left Molly to explain to him why she had to go, begging her to make Chris realise that her journey was really necessary and that she didn't want to leave. The woman comforted her, perturbed by the strained look on her face and the bleakness in her eyes. One night away from a husband, albeit a newly-wed one, seemed little enough reason for such grief.

Penny had not told the housekeeper everything. There were details she preferred to explain to Chris herself and there was still much she did not understand. From what Gerald had implied, she could only pray to be in time. Laura was dead. Nobody could hope to help Laura. Perhaps her baby could be saved, Gerald had said, the baby to whom life had been but a matter of weeks and whose mother had been a whole universe. Gerald had sounded calm about this with a detachment that amazed Penny, but his concern was all for Julie. In an orgy of grief, Julie had locked herself away, he'd said, and would see no one. They feared for her safety as, distressed beyond measure, she had already threatened suicide. Only Penny could help her Gerald had insisted.

"Come to her, Penny," he had pleaded. "Come at once before something dreadful happens. Oh God,

I cannot bear to think of it. Please come, Penny. Come and save us."

She didn't go for him. She went for Julie. What in Laura's death, the death of a woman she barely liked, could be driving Julie to suicide?

There was no pleasure in Penny's return to Avon House. Many of the staff, especially Jean and a subdued Rosa, welcomed her with relief, but the carefree atmosphere of the opening had gone. Penny was taken straight to Gerald and, if she'd expected to find him heartbroken, she was mistaken. He was as cool as the Gerald she'd first known in London. Looking at his studied elegance and face to face with him again, Penny waited for all the past wonder of her love for him to come rushing back to hold her. Nothing happened. It was as she had known before she left Alderbridge, Gerald Hart meant nothing to her now. She was free of the infatuation that had held her in its grip. Gerald came to greet her with a kiss as usual, but, as his hands lightly gripped her shoulders, she turned a cool cheek to him.

"Gerald, I was so sorry to hear your news. How is the baby?"

"About the same. I don't think they expect him to rally."

"Are you sure?"

"Practically. I don't know how to tell Julie if it happens. She's going through hell about it all."

"Julie going through hell — why?"

"Sit down, Penny, and I'll ring for some coffee then we'll talk."

"But I came to see Julie and I do have to get back tonight."

"Tonight? Does this husband of yours have you on chains?"

"No, but I like to be with him."

"Well, ours was a very modern marriage, Laura's and mine, as you know. Neither of us lay claim to the other. We lived our own lives."

He fell silent then. Laura's life, however free, was over. For a second both of them remembered her alive and vibrant, demanding and unfettered except by the pregnancy she'd resented, a pregnancy she'd deliberately invited to help her gain her own ends. Suddenly Penny realised that she might have courted her own death, too, as a means of getting her own way.

"What happened, Gerald? What really happened?"

He didn't pretend not to understand. There was no hesitation before he replied, "Laura found out about Julie and me."

"Julie and you?"

"Yes. You knew it was happening before you left."

"I didn't think it was so serious — just another of your affairs."

"Don't, Penny! Please! You and I were such fools to become engaged when we were both in love with someone else."

"Did you really love Laura, Gerald?" For the first time she felt a hint of sympathy for him.

"She gave my life the drive it needed. Laura was the force in me. Without her, there is nothing."

"Didn't you tell her? Why did you let a flirtation with Julie come between you?"

"It wasn't just a flirtation. Julie loved me, wildly, even fanatically, and I needed her too."

Penny remembered Julie's inheritance and knew just how Gerald had needed the poor deluded girl. He couldn't afford to let her fall out of love with him, any more than he had wanted to let go of Penny. Love to him was power. He had needed Julie's total dependence, a real commitment to him.

He must have sensed Penny's thoughts, for he continued, "Don't judge me too harshly, Penny. It isn't easy to be the puppet on the string. Laura manipulated me so completely that I needed my own doll."

"And once I was that?"

"I lost you, Penny. That little-girl bloom that ensnared me has gone.

You've become a woman. I almost envy him!"

"Don't!" Any comparison between Chris and this man sickened her. Chris had been the one firm touchstone when Gerald had tossed her in adolescent emotions. She forced the conversation back to Laura. "When Laura found out what did you do?"

"Do? I did nothing. It's always better to ride Laura's storms."

"And Julie?"

"There was a scene. Julie begged to be allowed to stay near me. Laura loved the power. She laughed, pretended she was going to take the baby and leave. 'Have him'! she said and drove away into the night. I can still hear her laughing now. It was the same laughter as when she told me to go ahead and marry you just before she tried to commit suicide. Penny, I know it was just her way of using the situation. She meant to come back. She meant to make us jump to her command. But, the car crashed. It wasn't bluff anymore. Now she's dead."

He sat with his head bowed as if the outburst had drained him. There was no emotion left in him and Penny, watching him, knew that he had always lived off the passions of others. Without Laura he would be like a shell. At least, until he found another relationship to give colour to his life. Would Julie be strong enough to carry him? Penny thought not. She was beginning to understand why Laura's death had upset Julie so much. She must be blaming herself for the accident, feeling that she was responsible. She voiced this opinion.

"Gerald, does Julie think the accident was her fault? Does she blame herself?"

"I suppose so. She won't talk about it. She's shut up in her room and won't see anybody."

"How can I help, then?"

"She'll see you. She asked for you over and over again. You can help both of us, Penny."

"Both of you?"

"Yes. Julie must go away. For her own sake and for mine."

"Still thinking of yourself, Gerald. How can she harm you?"

"The scandal, Penny. I've got things going now. I can't afford a scandal."

"And that's all that matters?"

"I care about Julie of course, but I can't let her ruin my whole career."

"You could marry her now. Her money would help, surely?" There was a sneer in Penny's voice and a curl to her lip, but Gerald didn't seem to notice.

"Later perhaps. But for now she must leave as soon as possible. There'll be talk if others realise how hysterical she is."

"And you could be blamed for Laura's death if she insists on blaming herself?"

"That mustn't happen. I must have time to grieve."

Time to be seen to grieve, Penny thought to herself, but she didn't say any more. She waited to be taken to

Julie and kept her feelings locked in her heart.

To her surprise Penny was let into Julie's room as soon as she spoke. Her voice was the key and, recognising it, Julie ran to unlock the door. She was so totally changed, so crumpled into numbness that Penny hardly recognised her. She was so pale, so breathless and so quivering with tension that Penny could only lead her to a low settee in the room and sit holding her while she shuddered with the intensity of her emotions.

"Penny," she said at last, "do you know why I wanted you? I had to tell you that I killed her."

"No, Julie!"

"Yes. A long time ago, I wanted to do it for you and now I've done it for myself."

A pitiful smile lit her face and Penny knew from the strangeness of her manner that the accident had caused some temporary delirium. Julie really believed that she'd killed Laura. She must have longed for her death so much.

"Will he marry me now, Penny, now that I have killed her?"

"Ssh!" Penny rocked the distracted girl in her arms. She dare not tell her that Gerald wanted her gone. Julie in return clung to her without a suspicion that she would be anything but her protector. She could not leave her yet. She must wait and try to persuade Julie to leave with her. In the meantime, she needed a doctor to help Julie and a telephone to reach Chris.

It was supper-time before she could leave Julie at all and then not for long. She tried to ring Chris, but there was no reply from Grange House. Ted answered from the Cottage, but he hadn't seen Chris and Penny knew of no real reason to ask him to seek out Chris. Molly would have explained. Instead, she told Ted all that she knew of Laura's death and its strange effect on Julie.

"Bring her here, Penny. Don't leave

her with him." Ted insisted so Penny and he arranged a harbour where Julie might recover. Then Penny dialled Grange House again, anxious to let Chris know she'd be home tomorrow. There was no reply then or any of the other times she tried that evening. In the morning the silence was still as absolute and, between packing and a doctor's visit, Penny didn't find time to ring again.

It was after lunch before she could set out with Julie heavily drugged in the back seat. She drove straight to Alderbridge and settled Julie in at the Cottage before going home. There was a calm acceptance about the other girl that suggested she was beginning the long, slow journey out of the tunnel of despair back to normality. Ted and June helped. They welcomed her, fussed over her and listened to the instructions the doctor had given Penny. All would be well now. Julie was in safe hands. Penny could go home to Chris. She was tired to the point of exhaustion, but happiness lightened her feet. She so longed to see him again. She wanted to be with him so much.

Grange House, when she returned, was strangely quiet, deserted almost. Penny ran from room to room, calling Chris. There was no reply. Not even Molly made her austere entrance at any doorway. What had happened? Where were they all? Chris was never as late as this. He should be here waiting for her, longing for her as much as she wanted him. She was in their bedroom before the full seriousness of the situation began to dawn on her. Flowers still filled the room and a stuffy sweetness clung to their scent. Nothing had changed since she left. There was even the white sheer nightie and wrap she'd chosen so lovingly thrown across the bed where she'd left it when Molly had knocked. On the dressing-table, she saw the note.

She was frantic. She could not open it until she'd sat down on the bed and then, for some reason, she jumped up and gathered all the flowers together and carried them into the bathroom. She dumped them in the bath then, returning to the bedroom, threw open the windows. She needed air. Where was Chris? Why wasn't he here? She knew the answer before her trembling fingers drew out his letter. She knew it instinctively. Chris had left her. Without the slightest warning, he had gone and he wasn't coming back. His letter confirmed her fears.

Dear Penny,

Why did you go to him? I came home expecting so much to find an empty house. Molly rang from her sister's to tell me. So, his wife was killed — how could you help?

It can only mean one thing — you wanted to be with him.

It hasn't worked out has it? I thought — any man would have thought — that by giving up all contact with my own past I could expect the same fidelity from you.

I thought you had settled down to our marriage. This weekend was so marvellous. Was it all a pretence? It was good for business, I know, but I cannot continue to live a lie. I cannot go on living with you without despising myself and, what is worse, despising you. How can we live together while you still fly to that man at the slightest provocation? Well, now he is free. Perhaps things will be different for you now. You may be able to be a perfect wife for him without the effort you apparently found such a strain for me. Was I so difficult to please, Penny? Why did you have to long to be able to make me happy when you and he can so easily find bliss?

I am going away. The firm needs a representative in Australia and I have volunteered. The contract is for a year, so it will give you time to get yourself sorted out.

I shan't see you again before I go. Perhaps I shall grow to think more kindly of you when I am away from you.

If you should have decided against Gerald by the time of my return, then we may be able to shake down together.

Thousands have done it for no better a reason than security! We could do it too.

But you must be free, Penny, to make this decision for yourself — no pressure this time. I never should have married you knowing what I did but I so wanted to give you a harbour, some happiness after such disillusion. I never dreamed that all would be for nothing at the first hint of his freedom. I pray that this time he will treat you better. I'm afraid he won't. How can he change?

If only I could have made you see his worthlessness.

Grow up, Penny, now — for God's sake! Does he have to die before you're free of him?

Stay at Grange House, please. I

have arranged an increased allowance for you through Mr. Limpeney. I shall not write but, if you need me, our solicitor will tell you how to contact me. If you are ill or want any thing, please go to him. I do not want any more anger or bitterness between us, Penny. Try to understand. If you want me, I will come to you but I shall not come unless you ask. When I return, it will be time enough to think of a divorce. Don't blame me for going away.

It is necessary. How silly I was in my happiness when I thought you loved me and me only. I beg of you now only one thing — if you want me, let me come to you.

Otherwise, let me stay far away and forget you were ever my wife.

CHRIS

"If you want me, let me come to you" — how funny! Penny sat contemplating that one line which, for her, stood out

340

from all the others, then suddenly she broke into laughter, a strange unnatural laugh that held no mirth. Between spasms of such hysteria, she talked aloud to Chris.

"If I want you! I cannot bear the loss of you. You'll never know how entirely I was unable to bear your not loving me, Chris. I never loved him at all compared with what I feel for you. He's done it! He has come between us and ruined our marriage. Why did you let him? Why did you believe I'd run to him? I didn't. I went for Julie. Didn't Molly explain? — but then she didn't really know.

Oh what a muddle! Why did you go away? — why, when I love you so? Of course, I want you. Please, please, come to me."

She threw herself across the bed, weeping. There was nothing else to do. It was too late to go to Mr. Limpeney. He would tell her how to find Chris, help her to convey how desperately she needed him, even teach her how to beg for his return. First thing in the morning she'd go down to his office. Everything must be all right. Fully clothed and on top of the bed she fell asleep and it was there that Molly found her when she returned to Grange House later that evening. Without any questions she helped her into bed and brought her hot milk. She could throw no light on Chris's reaction to Penny's absence the night before because she hadn't seen him. She'd phoned from her sister's to explain that Penny had been called away.

"Did he seem cross, Molly?"

"Cross? Why should he be? I told him how your friend's wife had been killed."

"Well, you see there's been a misunderstanding — some trouble — and he's gone away."

"Maybe he's gone to visit one of his friends."

"No. He's had to go to Australia for a month or two. No, that's a lie! He's gone for good. He's left me!"

Embarrassed at being the recipient of this confidence, Molly tried to comfort her young mistress.

"Don't you worry too much, dear. He'll be back. He knows when he's well off. If it was just a tiff, he'll think better of it."

"That's just it. There wasn't any tiff. He thinks I went back to Gerald. He doesn't trust me!"

Again, she burst into tears, but this time Molly was there to comfort her as she continued to do for the next few days. She wouldn't let Penny get up, but sent for the doctor who this time insisted on a week in bed. By the end of that week he had confirmed that she was pregnant. What was to have been her greatest joy was now a cause for further weeping.

"I can't. I don't want to," she shouted at the doctor amid her angry sobs. "You don't understand!" He understood far more than she realised but all he said was, "I'll prescribe a sedative for you. Try to rest now."

Rest! All that anybody thought of was rest. Their kindness and patience exasperated her beyond all reason. She was treated by Molly and her friends from the Cottage who came to her as something fragile and breakable. Time hung on her hands and she had too many hours for thought. Chris had abandoned her just when she needed him. How could she send for him now?

As soon as she was allowed out of her room she made her way down to the Cottage.

"I shan't throw a fit or break in two," she told Ted irritably when he expressed concern at her walking so far, the effort having made her breathless.

"I won't go back!" she announced suddenly as the idea came to her. Never to return to Grange House and see daily reminders of Chris would be so much better. She could stay here in the Cottage and have his child. Ted approved of the idea. June would be able to keep an eye on her and, God

344

knows, she needed watching. Almost as much as Julie. Before he agreed, though, he talked her into contacting Chris. "He ought to know, Penny. It's his baby as well as yours."

"He doesn't care! He despises me — he said so in his letter."

"Perhaps he was angry then. Give him a chance. Tell him about the baby at least."

"Why?"

"It's a bond between you. Let it help to heal the break."

"You mean he'll want me for the baby if not for myself?"

Even that chance she jumped at. Chris had been trembling on the brink of accepting her she was sure. If only she could recapture the chance to make their marriage work. She wouldn't ask for his love this time. Only his being with her, with her and the baby. Ted was right. Chris deserved to know about the baby. She'd find out his address from Mr. Limpeney and contact him right away.

The grey-haired solicitor smiled his slow wide smile when he gave Penny a phone number as well as the address.

"Good girl!" he approved though she had not told him why she wanted it. She felt safe with it in her handbag as if it were the key to her whole happiness. Strange then how for a whole evening, alone in her room, she sat studying the telephone. She had only to pick it up to hear Chris speak, but she couldn't bring herself to lift the receiver. It was midnight before she got through and her call was answered by a woman.

"Yes, this is Mr. Lloyd's suite. Who's speaking?" was the answer to her query of surprise at finding a woman in Chris's rooms.

"His wife."

"Oh, Penny! This is Joanna here. How nice to hear from you." Joanna! She was with Chris! In his room! At midnight! Jealousy burned her mind and seared her judgement. She couldn't speak, but she could hear muffled laughter on the line and the words,

"Darling, not now! Let me get rid of her first."

Get rid of her! Get rid of Penny, so that she'd be free for him? How dare she! The voice came again, clear now.

"Penny? Are you still there? Chris is in the bath at the moment. Can I take a message or will you ring back?"

No, she wouldn't call back. Let him do the begging."

"Tell him I called. No, there's no message — only, tell him I'm staying at the Cottage if he wants to get in touch."

"I'll tell him." Another giggle hastily stifled before she said: "Are you sure that's all?"

"Quite sure."

Penny put down the receiver. So that was that! Believing she'd gone to Gerald, Chris had gone straight back to Joanna. They were together now. She couldn't bear to think of it. What on earth could she do?

By morning the solution had come to her. She and Julie were in the same boat, heartbroken and alone. There was only one remedy. Work. Julie was already wavering about setting up in business on her own. She just lacked the initiative to get started. Well, Penny had been in at the start of two enterprises; she could give her the push she needed. Together, they'd launch a new hotel. Julie wanted to go to London and that suited Penny. She'd get as far away from Alderbridge as possible. She couldn't bear the thought of staying here now. There were too many memories.

Both girls threw themselves into the project, burying their feelings for the sake of its success. Penny found London noisy and stuffy through that long summer, but she was glad to work each day until she fell asleep from sheer tiredness. She taught Julie all she knew, as if in building her up she could find some peace with herself. Some good had to come out of Gerald's friendship, all couldn't be ashes. To the baby, at first she gave no thought. It wasn't that she wanted to get rid of it, but that it survived in spite of her industry. In fact, it thrived on Penny's hard work and she began to feel a bond of admiration for this sturdy seed that refused to be neglected. She wouldn't give way to depression. They said that babies sensed a mother's mood. Let this one know determination in the womb. Chris had said grow up. Well, she'd done that. Never again would she need a man to lean on. She'd make a life for the baby on her own and she'd see that it was a good one. No more anger or bitterness — a child needed to grow up without either.

By Christmas she was heavy with the baby but not ready to give in to her weariness. Her parents begged her to go home to them for the festival but she didn't want Alderbridge without Chris. She had no heart for the festivities or for the gay challenge of the shops. She bought her Christmas gifts early and sent them with a letter she didn't know was sad at heart. An unbearable vision of herself and Chris in the sitting-room of Grange House before a huge log-fire in the days when his mother and father were alive pierced her heart. She threw herself blindly into preparations for Julie's Christmas, not wanting to be alone with her thoughts. By the New Year it was obvious that Julie was on the up and up and ready to go it alone. At last, Penny turned her thoughts to the arrival of the baby and was surprised how much she wanted to be with her mother. All the love of her own childhood came rushing back and she knew the time had come to go home.

The snowdrops were just thrusting their brave whiteness into the face of the February storms when Penny's baby was born. When the pain was at its worst her heart called out for Chris.

"I love you, Chris. I love you and you'll never know it." Thought of him strengthened her and their daughter was born to the repeated profession of her mother's love: "I love you! I love you!"

What a pity, thought the sensitive young nurse who wheeled her back to her ward, that the husband wasn't here to hear his wife's declaration. How could he have missed such a moment!

A fortnight later, Penny and her baby occupied one of the best rooms that the Cottage had to offer. They could have returned to her mother in the village, but Penny wanted to keep her new independence. Working for Julie had left her in funds so she could afford the Cottage without reducing its profits or touching the allowance Chris had left. She had calculated it all carefully. She could afford to enjoy all the pleasures of motherhood for the first six months, then she must think again. At the moment, she was so tired that all she wanted to do was sleep. She still clung to the habit learned in hospital of an afternoon rest because it brought oblivion. The peace and quietness of the room made her relax a little. She sank back against the pillows and tried to tell herself that she would be happy again. Chris would come back — and in her dreams he did.

She awoke from a sleep in which Chris lay beside her, warm in the big soft bed, to find that someone had opened her door. The pale wintry sun had moved from the window, so she knew she had slept long.

"Sorry," she murmured sleepily to the figure who came across to her side and set a tray on her bedside table.

"Is it tea-time already?" There was no answer and Penny sat up suddenly, aware of the strange silence.

"Chris!"

Her voice made only a thread of sound. He stood looking down at her, his gaze taking in her fragile pallor and the dark lines under her eyes. And then he was kneeling beside the bed, his arms trying to engulf her.

"My darling! My precious Penny! What is it? Whatever happened to you?"

The soft touch of his lips against her hair made her realise, as if for the first time, that this was real. It was actually happening. Chris had come back to her. She had wanted him with such intensity that she almost felt she must be still dreaming. He felt the quiver go through her and, looking down into her face, said:

"Penny, tell me everything. I have suffered every kind of fear today."

"Suffered?"

"Oh, my darling little echo! How lovely to hear your voice repeating my words again. Just like you used to. Penny, I love you so. I've fought against it but I love you so much."

Instinctively, her hand went out to him and he drew her very gently closer to him.

"I've always loved you, Penny, ever since I rescued you from the swans. I've loved everything about you — your gentleness, your determination, your innocence. And yet you drove me mad with jealousy — when I thought of you with that fellow Gerald, I could have killed you."

A smile brought light to her tired face. "I — I thought you despised me."

"Penny, I want you with all my heart and soul. I cannot live without you. I came back to tell you so, to try again, but they said you were in hospital."

"I came home today."

"I know. I went to the hospital. Penny, what's wrong? Nobody will tell me. They all say it would be better if I heard it from you. What is it, Penny? Let me look after you now. I don't deserve you, but you are mine! Mine for always! You belong to me. Tell me the truth. There can be no more pretence between us now."

So he didn't know! A shyness that was in itself a delight crept over her. He watched the colour come into her face just as the first cries came from the tiny dressing room.

"Go and see, Chris. I'm not ill. It's

just that now there is someone else who wants me."

The cries grew shrill as he crossed to the other room. "Bring her to me, Chris."

"Penny, I can't!"

Laughing softly to see his amazement and complete lack of control Penny slipped out of bed and fetched her daughter herself. Back in the double bed, the soft little head nuzzled into her breast. In the knowledge of Chris's newly declared love, she felt no hesitation in helping the tiny mouth find its satisfaction. But Chris who had first gone white, now coloured and turned away.

"Chris darling!" she chided. "It's your daughter. Don't look away. She must come first for a while."

He turned back and Penny saw that there were tears in his eyes.

"It's not that. Seeing you then made me realise how much I've missed you. How much you've gone through alone! Why didn't you tell me, Penny?"

"I tried, but Joanna was with you. Didn't she give you my message?"

"She never said a word. I swear I never knew you'd been in touch. But then Joanna was so wrapped up in her new husband all this trip, following one another around all cuddling and kissing."

"Even in your room at midnight?" Penny asked quietly, her whole happiness depending on his answer.

"Penny, what do you mean? You think that Joanna and I? Yes you do! But I had to have some pride. All right, I'll admit I used her to make you jealous but I was in hell over Gerald."

"And in your room when I phoned? What was she doing laughing and cooing as I called?"

"I don't know what you're talking about!"

Then, light dawned and he asked very gently, "Penny, what time did you ring?"

"I told you. At midnight. How could I ever forget!"

"The time in Australia, my Penny Precious, was ten in the morning."

"Ten in the morning!"

"Yes, my precious echo. Joanna and her lapdog would have been waiting for their assignment for that day. I suppose I was showering and she took the call in my sitting-room. But why didn't she tell me? I'll kill her for that!"

"Chris, do you mean you and she were never — "

"Lovers?" he spoke the word that had stuck in her throat. "No. Before I married you, I wasn't a saint, my darling, but since then I've wanted only you. I tried to forget you, but I couldn't. I came back to beg you to try again."

He was drawing her closer but the movement disturbed the baby who yelled in protest.

"You'll have to wait, Chris. Tina needs me."

"I need you too," he said with such emphasis that she saw the full wonder of their love. Their daughter's head fell sleepily away from the breast and Penny transferred her carefully into her father's arms.

"She's yours, darling. Tina — for Christina — after you."

He put his other arm closely round Penny and said, "I've got two girls to look after now."

"Our knight in shining armour?"

"No. She'll find her own in due course. And I haven't been much of a knight to you."

"I'm not complaining. Take us home, Chris, please."

There were no more questions and no more explanations. They could come later. Now, there was only love, a love big enough to engulf the three of them and later leave plenty to spare for Tina's brothers and sisters.

WITH SOMEBODY ELSE
Theresa Charles

Rosamond sets off for Cornwall with Hugo to meet his family, blissfully unaware of the shocks in store for her.

A SUMMER FOR STRANGERS
Claire Hamilton

Because she had lost her job, her flat and she had no money, Tabitha agreed to pose as Adam's future wife although she believed the scheme to be deceitful and cruel.

VILLA OF SINGING WATER
Angela Petron

The disquieting incidents that occurred at the Vatican and the Colosseum did not trouble Jan at first, but then they became increasingly unpleasant and alarming.

DOCTOR NAPIER'S NURSE
Pauline Ash

When cousins Midge and Derry are entered as probationer nurses on the same day but at different hospitals they agree to exchange identities.

A GIRL LIKE JULIE
Louise Ellis

Caroline absolutely adored Hugh Barrington, but then Julie Crane came into their lives. Julie was the kind of girl who attracts men without even trying.

COUNTRY DOCTOR
Paula Lindsay

When Evan Richmond bought a practice in a remote country village he did not realise that a casual encounter would lead to the loss of his heart.

ENCORE
Helga Moray

Craig and Janet realise that their true happiness lies with each other, but it is only under traumatic circumstances that they can be reunited.

NICOLETTE
Ivy Preston

When Grant Alston came back into her life, Nicolette was faced with a dilemma. Should she follow the path of duty or the path of love?

THE GREEN PUMA
Margaret Way

Catherine's time was spent looking after her father's Queensland farm. But what life was there without David, who wasn't interested in her?